THE SPIRIT IN THE FOLD

A HISTORICAL TIME SLIP MYSTERY

JANE THORNLEY

RIVERFLOW PRESS 2022

FOREWORD

I have always dreamed of holding a conversation with someone from the past. What would we talk about? How would the evolution of our thinking clash? In part, *The Spirit in the Fold* was born from just such a desire but it also emerged from the prologue of *The Florentine's Secret*, book three in *The Agency of the Ancient Lost and Found* historical mystery thriller series. There are subtle differences between the two. If you don't notice them, I won't point them out.

In any case, each book in that series begins with a prologue set in the historical time period which drives Phoebe McCabe's exploits. In *The Florentine's Secret*, Gabriela, the seamstress to the Medici family emerged fully formed and demanded that her story be told. Sometimes characters claim so much attention in an author's brain that they must be set free. Thus, Gabriela came alive.

Just as this novel is connected to *The Agency of the Ancient Lost and Found* series, so too is it linked to the *Time Shadows* series, of which this is volume two. In the *Time Shadows* series, each story is based on the premise that we have all lived previous lives and that sometimes these lives intersect with our own . Whether you believe in reincarnation or not, it is a fascinating concept for an author.

lorence, Italy
March 1477

SHE MUST REMAIN focused on pinning the fabric—velvet the color of birds' eggs or those tiny blue flowers that first bloom in spring—at the lady's shoulders, careful not to add unnecessary bulk. "Ladies must never appear to carry weight even when they are with child," her father had warned. "Ensure that the profile remains lean until below the waist and only then release the fabric's flow."

This lady was small and slim so that no amount of fabric would likely ruin her profile despite the child she carried high in her belly. The velvet gamurra would spill down in one fluid length as befitting a lady of wealth in the Republic of Florence. And the sleeves! She could not wait to see those beautiful wing-like creations tied in place. For this family, they Republic's regulators would look the other way.

"What is your name, girl?" the lady asked suddenly.

The question startled her so that she nearly dropped her purse of pins. "Gabriela di Domenico, my lady." Her voice came out small and faint, more like the breeze whispering in the curtains than her true voice. Her deft fingers continued pinning, careful not to prick the flesh or cause a moment's discomfort, but she was more distracted now.

"Look at me."

Slowly Gabriela lifted her gaze, something she had been told not to do: never meet the gaze of your betters; never permit your eyes to stare around at the richness of their houses; never speak until you are spoken to. It had taken everything she possessed to obey that decree in this particular house and often she failed. She was not, she had been told, an obedient girl.

"I know your surname, child. You are under my roof with your father, but you are so young. It disturbs me that you work so hard when the hour is late. The clock has already struck nine hours," Lady de' Medici said. "I look at you and see a girl only a few years older than my eldest daughter and yet all of my children are now in their beds where they belong. You are away from yours much later than I would ever permit."

Because I must work to survive, my lady. Why do the rich never realize that? Not that her father was poor, but whatever they gained, they earned because they worked hard. "I have lived a full fourteen years, my lady, almost a woman."

"Hardly a woman yet not quite a child. What does your mother think of you being out so late?" the lady asked.

Gabriela stepped away, folded her hands in front of her, and studied the carpet below her feet—rich blocks of red in varying hues fitting into one another like her father's favorite puzzle pieces. Beautiful. Her father would call the design "Eastern." "My mother remains in her bed, my lady. I am expecting a brother or a sister within the month."

"Oh, how very blessed you are! God truly shines upon your family as every child born is a gift. Is this your first sibling?"

Gabriela struggled to suppress her anxiety. Mama's pregnancy did not seem such a blessing. She had not been well these past months and the midwife feared hers would be another difficult birth. Two babies lost already, blood drenching the linens in a red more vibrant than found in any carpet, the color of life bleeding into death. She could not bear the thought of that hue staining their lives once again.

"Look at me, I said. How often do you pray, girl?"

She lifted her gaze. "As many times as I can, my lady." Which was not often. There was always too much to do to spend precious hours in prayer. She was certain God would understand.

The woman's face brightened by a faint smile. It was a good face, Gabriela realized, with an unblemished complexion and features pleasant to look at. The mother of the great Lorenzo de' Medici had chosen her son's bride well, her father had remarked, and truly, there was kindness there. "It is good to pray often. Come, we will pray for your mother now, but first remove this gown. You must return tomorrow, the day after, and the day after that to continue the work so that these garments will be ready for Easter. My daughters require new apparel also. They grow so quickly."

Though Easter was yet many weeks away, there was much work to be done to prepare the family for the celebration. Giorneas and cioppas in silk and velvets, all of which must be sent to furriers, embroiderers, and other craftsmen to complete the outfit, would take much time, though they did much in-house. And the sleeves! She would love to fashion those herself but Father and his journeymen tailors would not let her yet touch them. They were the crown of an outfit and closely regulated by the republic, though Father often broke the rules, to his clients' delight.

While her father fitted the men, she would tend the ladies as the family preferred. The Medici alone brought their house more custom than they could often manage, especially now with her mother's illness. There was little time for prayer except on Sundays and feast days. Gabriela reined in her worries. "Be careful, my lady. The pins are long and fierce."

The lady laughed. "'Long and fierce.' Oh, Gabriela di Domenico, you have such a way with words—a seamstress poet. Bianca, come help the girl."

"Yes, my lady." The servant, Bianca, emerged from the shadows where she had been watching and assisted Gabriela while the lady stepped out of the carefully pinned gown. Gabriela swore that the glances Bianca shot her were sharper than the pins but she could not understand why. What had she done? Surpassed her station with her cleverness? Had not Mama warned her?

The long-faced maid laid the dress upon the bed before draping a green silk velvet robe over her mistress's shoulders.

"Not the velvet, Bianca. Bring me the gold woolen one and be quick about it for I am chilled."

"Shall I close the shutters, my lady?" Bianca asked while lifting a thick saffron-colored robe from the trunk.

That had been Gabriela's first completed piece. Her father had cut the fabric and she had worked the seams in perfect little stitches, adding the tiny leaves embroidered along the hem on a whim when she could find the time. Her mother had been working then so Gabriela had stolen the necessary moments to compete the task, but what a tongue-lashing she had received! Mama had chastised her for wasting time on such details until Father had intervened, pleased with her skills. *But she is not an embroiderer,* her mother had said, *and the Lady Medici requested a plain yellow robe and will only pay for such.* But Mama was wrong. Gabriela's cheeks flushed with pride.

"Leave the window." Lady Medici took Gabriela's hand and led her toward the corner where the fire burned and blue velvet stools sat before the cross on the wall—and such a cross! Gabriela had not seen anything of its like except in the cathedral where the paintings and sculptures always struck her dumb with wonder. This one seemed to shimmer with light and color, every detail rendered with perfection, Christ's agony so lifelike that the sight of His wounds caused her soul to bleed. Was she permitted to stare?

"Keep your head bowed, girl."

She dropped her gaze, ashamed that she had been caught regarding the blessed Jesus so brazenly. Together the Lady de' Medici knelt with her and prayed, Gabriela understanding the words, though they were all in Latin. She was not supposed to know the Latin her father had taught her. That knowledge must be kept hidden, too, as was what Mama called her "strident" ways. Bold, unfeminine, sinful, prone to do things not her role to do. How many times had she heard this?

Maybe she should pray harder for her soul, but that night she prayed only for her mother, not in Latin but simply in the language of her thoughts. *Please, Jesus, keep Mama safe. Do not let there be more blood. Let my bother or sister enter the world safely...*

They remained there for a long time but for how long Gabriela was uncertain. She only knew that her knees grew sore, every bone in her body crying out to move, and that precious time was slipping by. The clock struck ten hours.

"Mistress, please rest now. You must not tire yourself or the baby," Bianca cautioned.

Lady de' Medici lifted her head and turned. "Yes, that is true. Where is my husband, Bianca?"

"Downstairs with the men, my lady."

"As always, always with the men," she sighed as Bianca helped her to her feet. "No doubt they discuss pagan tales and read poetry. Are all others in our household in for the night?"

"I know not, my lady, for I have been upstairs with you these last few hours."

"Yes, of course. Pray tell my husband that I have gone to bed and send this girl downstairs to await her father. Make sure she gets a bit of warm milk for it is too late an hour to be beyond her own roof."

"Yes, my lady."

Gabriela glanced at the velvet gamurra across on the bed. She really must take that with her. In the hours before they returned, she could sew the seams. She made to take it but Bianca nudged her into the corridor. "Leave it. She is weary. Wait here until I attend my mistress. I will return to take you down-stairs soon."

"But I must take the giornea with me tonight," she whispered.

"Wait, I said. Do not move and do not touch a thing." The door clicked shut behind her.

Gabriela stood gazing down the long hall, a hall almost as big as the Santa Maria del Fiori's aisles and almost as richly decorated, too. So many doors. How could so few people live inside so many rooms? These walls could house all of her aunts and uncles plus their children and animals, as well. Her house was large enough but this was enormous.

She took a step forward. A white marble statue of a nude man stood midway down. He appeared to be holding a shield in one hand and a spear in the other. A soldier, then. Never had she seen a nude man in the flesh, though she knew what they must look like from the statues. But how strange. Would it not make more sense for a soldier to go into battle fully clothed? He seemed vulnerable in his nakedness, especially *there*.

So accustomed was she of thinking in terms of apparel that she began to mentally dress the statue, adding every piece of clothing that she knew he might need. Had she not sewn every type of item with her very fingers at one time or another? In her father's house, everyone worked the trade.

First came the undershirt in fine linen to wear over the man's hose, for he must have hose as no man went without. Next, the torso's close-fitting farsetto, which, since the man was a soldier, must be quilted to protect his vitals—no, wait. Velvet would be all wrong. Instead, she replaced her silken imaginings with a sturdier leather suitable for battle, after which came the tunic, again in leather, something in which the man could move and wield his sword. Maybe she should emboss it with gold mail as befitting a soldier from a noble house. She swung her arm about as if holding a sword to better understand how the fabric should move. It must be pleated, she decided, with a gusset applied under each arm.

Men's voices in the hall below interrupted her musings. Scuffling sounds, a door slamming.

"They roam the streets, master," someone called. "They seek any from the House of Medici—servant, scribe, noble—to harass with abandon!"

"Ruffians all! How dare they lay hands on you, Marcus! Were you alone?"

Gabriela peered over the banister to the hall below. Two men stood there, one handsome with wavy black hair dressed in a crimson velvet cloak lined with fur, the other clearly a servant by the looks of his drab blue but expertly tailored blue mantello. Blood oozed from a gnash at the servant's temple.

"Yes, sir. Lucas went into an alehouse while I continued on without him but, master, please do not go out tonight, even in company. The streets are plagued by thugs."

A door flew open and out stepped another man. Short, straight brown hair, a rich red velvet tunic of her father's making. In a raspy voice he said: "What happened, Giuliano?"

Gabriela slipped toward the top of the stairs and crouched low to improve her view. From this angle she could see her father stepping out from the room behind the great Lorenzo de' Medici, along with another man who wore a black tunic of her father's workmanship. That was the Medici children's tutor, the man her father called Poliziano but whom she must refer always as Master Angelo Ambrogini.

"Our people are being assaulted on the streets now, Lorenzo," replied the handsome one she knew to be Giuliano de' Medici, the younger Medici brother, "by hired thugs, is my guess. This is not the first time I've heard such tales but this is the first time they dared strike. Let us send our men out immediately to round up this scourge and punish them for this insult to our house!" The younger Medici was clearly in a fury, his cheeks as red as his cloak.

"And start a war?"

"But we *are* at war, brother."

"Calm yourself," said the raspy-voiced Magnifico stepping forward with his hands lifted, a ruby ring glinting on his middle finger. The great Lorenzo de' Medici. So strange that one so mighty should have a voice like chalk grinding over stone and a nose crushed as if that stone had rammed his face at birth. "We have no proof that Marcus was assaulted by our enemies when there are always thieves and brigands roaming the streets after dark."

"Not so, brother, for these thugs cried out: 'There goes Medici scum!' before attacking Marcus. Our crest gives us away. We cannot permit this assault to go unpunished."

"Nothing is to be solved by force until all avenues off diplomacy have been tested." The Magnifico turned toward the servant. "Marcus, go to the kitchen and have Roberto rouse the doctor to tend to your head. I will speak with you later. Brother, please join me in the library where we may talk in private."

He then addressed her father and the other man. "Domenico and Poliziano, pardon this interruption but our poetry reading must wait another time. Feel free to go about your business." With that, the two brothers stepped into the room and shut the door behind them.

Gabriela crept down the stairs.

"The Pazzis are behind this," Poliziano said to her father. "As sure as I am standing here, they are paying street ruffians to harass anyone wearing the Medici crest and all those who serve them while chewing away at their support in the republic."

"Surely they would not dare," her father insisted as Gabriela crossed the long marble hall. "The people of Florence are not such fools as that. The guilds know full well how trade has improved since the Medici came to power."

"But remember, Domenico, the pope himself is against this house, which will bear weight with some. Perhaps you and your daughter should stay the night? There is always room."

She stopped within steps of the men, hoping someone would acknowledge her.

"Not possible. I must be home, for my wife has not been well."

"Suit yourself. I will be away to my quarters to study. Safe travels." The man strode down the long hall toward the back of the building as if he hadn't seen Gabriela when she knew that he had.

"Who are the Pazzi?" Gabriela asked as her father turned toward her, "and why would the pope be against the great Medici? Do they not attend mass like everyone else?"

"Come, Gabriela, no time to talk now. Take your cloak. We must be home within the hour or your mother will fret. Do you have the dress?"

"It is upstairs in the lady's quarters. Should I run up and fetch it?"

"No time and I do not have my pieces, either, but no matter, we must be away." He paused to gaze around the hall, looking for a servant to saddle their mares and bring them around, but none were in sight. "We will go to the stables ourselves."

The stables were on the other side of the palazzo across the courtyard, a route they knew well. Tonight, they strode out across the garden with the trees whispering in the breeze overhead and the torches flickering, without speaking a word. It was a place in which she always longed to linger but never could. Tonight they half ran.

The stables were empty but for the soft snuffling of the horses, at least twenty in this section alone. Lorenzo de' Medici's own white stallion whinnied as they passed, stomping in his stall as if ready to be off. Their own two brown mares stood tied side by side at the end. At least they had been watered and fed.

They quickly saddled their mounts and led them to the outer stable doors and across the gravel to the back walls. The stone, lit by torches, climbed far over their heads and was guarded by a huge towering wooded gate at least one hand thick.

"Gatekeeper, let us out! It is I, the tailor Francisco di Domenico, and his daughter, bound to our home this night!" Her father called while gesturing for Gabriela to mount her ride as he swung into his own saddle.

The crunch of gravel behind them announced the gatekeeper, an old man with long gray hair and a thick beard wearing the Medici livery. "You are a brave one to venture out this night. The ruffians surround the palazzo where our men stand guard but they have been ordered not to engage in combat even if taunted. If you go out there, no one will protect you, tailor man."

"Regardless, we must be off. Open the gates."

"Your funeral." The gates swung open, revealing two liveried men standing in the torchlight beyond. No ruffians in sight, though Gabriela was unsure how to recognize them. It might be any citizen about this hour. Nothing could be seen in the shadows beyond, in any case. Still, her heart pounded in her ears.

Her father clicked his tongue and thumped his legs against old Francesca's side, prompting the mare to bolt. Chiara followed, eager to be off, the younger horse loving nothing better than a good run. And run they did, straight out of the gates and down the street, their hooves beating against the cobbles. Handfuls of men scattered from their path, some calling obscenities, and yet nothing broke their stride.

Across the Piazza della Signoria they galloped, Gabriela's veins pumping with excitement. Here they were running in the torchlight, people in little groups standing by the buildings, whispering at the street corners. The della Signoria building itself seemed to have a torch burning in every bracket. It was thrilling to be out so late!

The quickest route home was straight down Via del Vecchio and along the river, as they lived close to the Chiesa di Ognissanti on the other side of town —at least a half hour's ride.

"Father, why this route?"

"Safer!" he cried. "Too many brigands gather around the city walls!"

But this way would take longer, she knew, and not all the streets would be lit this late in the evening. Just when she thought to suggest a quicker path, she heard pounding hooves and swung around to see five mounted men barreling toward them.

"They are upon us!" she called, but whether her father heard she could not tell, for at that moment two other horsemen swerved in front of her, causing Chiara to rear up.

One man secured the mare's reins while another yanked Gabriela from the saddle. It all happened so quickly.

"Father, run!" she cried, kicking and screaming. But it was too late. Even as she struggled in the men's arms, her father was being set upon by five men, one of them yelling: "Medici scum!"

"I am but a tailor!" cried her father as fists and staves beat down about his head.

Gabriela kicked one of her attackers in the groin and, the moment he released her, swung around and kneed the other in the gut. Neither expected such fierceness in a girl, nor did those besetting her father expect to have that same girl jump upon one of their backs to grab his throat.

2

Florence, Italy
January 2022

"Let my father go! He has done nothing wrong, nothing!"

Crying and screaming, she kicked and scratched as one thug pulled her off her father's attacker while another bound her hands in shackles. There were strange flashing lights everywhere and she could no longer see her father struggling. "Father!" she cried. "Where are you?"

Two men were shoving her into a box now—a white, glossy-skinned box with a warm interior and bars along one wall. Baffled, she stared out. Still in the Piazza della Signoria but why did it appear so different? Why were so many people dressed in strange costumes? Why no horses? Where was her father?

The ruffians were all dressed in matching dark clothing with even stranger peaked hats. Nothing made sense. Lifting her hands, she stared at the shiny silver cuffs that bound her wrists before gazing dumbstruck at the streets flying by. A dream, this must be a wicked, wicked dream…

Minutes, maybe hours, later she found herself wrapped in a blanket sitting on a padded bench in a room with a cold white light blazing down from above. A woman wearing the same dark livery as the men, a red stripe running down long breeches, face partially covered by an odd blue mask, entered the chamber to offer her a bottle of water and an odd cup of something hot and dark. When she went to sip the water, it shocked her to find the same strange mask across her own mouth and nose.

"You may lift the mask to drink," the woman said, remaining several steps away.

She pulled the mask from her face and took the bottle, puzzled to find it soft and flexible like leather only clear. Could leather be made clear? She drank eagerly.

"What is your name and address?" asked the woman, the eyes above the mask wary. Her accent seemed equally strange—Italian yet not.

"Gabriela," she replied, surprised to hear her voice so deep. "Gabriela di Domenico. Where is my father? I do not know the word 'address.'" What happened to her throat?

"Where do you *live*?" the woman clarified.

"Oh, on the Via Borgo Ognissanti." Really? Why couldn't she picture her house?

"Why were you in the Piazza della Signoria, Signorina Domenico?"

She hesitated, staring at the woman's bodice with its gold buttons and her tight striped leggings—no giornea, no cloak, and such an odd design. Why couldn't she remember being in the piazza?

"Um, I, was returning from…" From where? "From the Medici palazzo," she continued with confidence. "Yes, my father, who is a tailor, and I were staying late to fit the family for the Easter celebrations and were beset by ruffians who pulled us from our mounts. Is my father unharmed? Where is he?"

"The Medici?" the woman asked incredulously.

Gabriela stared. "Yes, the Medici. Lorenzo the Magnifico…" Surely everyone knew the Medici? A stab of cold seared through her, not because she was afraid but because she suddenly realized how wrong everything was, horribly, horribly wrong. "Oh, my God," she whispered. "What is happening to me?"

"That is what we are attempting to discover," said the woman. "I can only say that you attacked two tourists and later assaulted a police officer in the Piazza della Signoria. You carry no identification and are dressed in nothing but nightclothes, or at least I believe that is what you wear. Are you under the care of a doctor?"

She looked down at her bare legs, at her red, raw feet, at the short white fabric sticking out from under the blanket. A man opened the door and requested that the woman step out, which she did, leaving Brooke alone in the room. *Brooke*, not *Gabriela*.

It was happening again, this time more vividly, more violently. Returning to Florence had been a terrible mistake and yet the only hope for salvation she had.

Shivering uncontrollably, somehow she managed to bring the styrofoam cup to her lips. Damn, that bitter brew tasted good. Gripping the cup with trembling hands, she waited for the images in her mind to settle down, forcing herself back into this century even while Gabriela's emotions still roiled away in her chest. *Gabriela, you are closer to me now than ever but you cannot continue to control my life.*

"Brooke?"

She looked up. There stood her friend Enrico, dear Enrico, dressed in some kind of leather coat over his silk pajama bottoms, his feet in those monogramed slippers he preferred, looking bewildered, anxious, and half-asleep above his mask. "Brooke Carter, what the hell is going on?"

She stood. "Enrico, forgive me. I didn't expect this to happen so soon or so...so unexpectedly. I—I wanted time to explain to you both but I got in so late and I thought it best to just rest and—" Her flight from Toronto to Rome had been delayed, causing her to miss her connection to Florence, and by the time she finally landed, it was already past eleven. Jet lag knocked her for a loop. She thought everything could wait until morning but clearly she had underestimated Gabriela.

He stepped forward, two officers at his heels. "You left the flat and ended up in the Piazza della Signoria in your nightclothes where you began attacking people—seriously?"

Oh, hell. Had she really done that? She glanced at the officers and back to Enrico. "That wasn't me. I mean, it was but it wasn't. I need to explain."

"Best you do, but first we have to keep you out of a padded cell. They want to place you in a doctor's care, do you understand?" He spoke in terse English, probably hoping that the Italian officers wouldn't understand. "The only thing stopping them is that you're a Canadian national and they aren't set up to help mentally ill visiting foreigners, especially in the age of Covid. Felix is on the phone now trying to talk his way out of this. We may have to engage a lawyer."

Felix, Enrico's partner in all possible ways as well as the other half of her two dearest friends, had always been the most sympathetic of the pair. Both knew more about her affliction than anybody, yet knew nothing at all, since she had only begun to understand what was happening herself.

"I'm not mentally ill, at least not in the traditional sense." Though how she could explain what was happening in a way that someone could accept? It took all she had not to break down. "Anyway, I'm hoping with your names holding so much weight around here, they'll set me free." The House of Riccio was one of the top design houses in all of Europe and revered in Florence. In this country of designers, her native sons were practically canonized. Still, it was a big ask, a huge ask.

Enrico sighed and stood by the bench beside her, folding his gloved hands before him while keeping his gaze fixed on the two officers. "You told us you were better," he whispered, still in English.

"I am," she said, "but it's complicated. I couldn't just explain everything on Zoom. I needed to come in person." And to regain her life once and for all.

"There are emails, phone calls. We would have appreciated some warning."

"I'm sorry," she whispered. She should have told them but she had been so afraid they would refuse. Desperation ruled her these days.

The door opened and another officer poked his head in, saying that she was free to go. Felix had worked his magic.

Enrico and Brooke were escorted into another area where more polizia stood, each person watching her as if she might leap at their throats at any moment. A lean, elegant man dressed in the most exquisite pale blue cashmere coat stood talking to a uniformed individual who must be the captain.

"Felix!" she cried.

Turning, he enveloped her in one of his famous hugs, the cashmere like a kiss against her skin.

"Be careful, Felix," whispered Enrico, "that blanket is probably crawling with disgusting multilegged things."

"Oh, my God, Brooke, what have you got yourself into now?" Felix whispered in English. "You look like, shit, by the way. What in hell is it that you wear?" He held her at arm's length. "Practically nothing. Drop that filthy blanket at once. You have no idea where that thing has been. *Presto.*" In seconds, he had removed his coat and draped it around her shoulders as if she were a queen rather than some crazy Canadian. That left him standing in his purple silk pajamas, daring the officers to so much as blink, which they clearly would never do, being totally starstruck to have the famed Felix Ferri standing in their midst.

With no further commentary from the carabinieri, she was bundled out of the station and into the waiting car that was left double-parked next to the curb with its lights flashing. Once inside the warm cocoon of plush leather with the streets flying past, she closed her eyes. One glance outside might become another trigger. She couldn't risk it.

"The polizia claim you were speaking some kind of strange version of Italian again," Felix said from beside her in the back seat while Enrico took the wheel up front, "and asking for your father, who you claimed was 'beset upon by ruffians' or some such thing. I do love that language, by the way. It is like you are acting in a play."

"In a way I am," she acknowledged. A terrible, bloody play.

"But your father has been gone for nearly a decade, correct? I recall that you needed to fly home for his funeral while you were studying here all those years ago," said Enrico, glancing in the rearview mirror at her. He had been careful not to touch her, she noticed, while Felix gripped her hand as if she might sink into a hole otherwise.

"Of course her father is gone, Rico. We know this. Brooke, as soon as we are home, we will ask you to explain everything and to hold nothing back. It is time to stop hiding things."

"I presume you have stopped taking your medication again," said Enrico in that voice he used when keeping a minor explosion at bay. His temper was legendary.

"It's resolution I need, not drugs, Enrico, and all the psychologists in the world can't cure what plagues me," she explained. She really didn't want to get into this here but he was leaving her no choice. "Once I weaned myself off those numbing medications, I finally began to uncover the truth, the *real* truth. That's why I'm here: to lay Gabriela to rest at last."

"Lay Gabriela to rest? You have a name now? Does that mean you are, what, possessed?" Enrico again.

"Not in the traditional sense, no," she said, trying to remain calm.

"Then explain yourself!"

"Do not push, Enrico." Felix shot his partner a warning glance in the rearview mirror.

"I will explain," she told them, "but try to keep an open mind."

The car eased to a stop on Via Gallo outside their apartment building where they waited until the electronic gates swung open and they could enter the courtyard. Once torches had lit those same walls, glowed in this very same courtyard. She could almost see them superimposed across her vision. Somehow this place had featured in Gabriela's life 545 years earlier.

"I warn you, you won't find it easy to accept," Brooke said as they entered the elevator. "It took a hell of a long time for me to get my head around it, but once I did, it all made sense." She fixed on the brass doors all the way to the top floor inside that tiny, claustrophobic elevator. "Just know one thing: I'm not insane."

As the doors hushed open, Felix shoved back the bronze gates and ushered her into the marble foyer of the flat occupying the entire top floor of this once-upon-a-time palazzo. "We will eagerly hear all you have to say, darling Ruscello." He was back to calling her by his favorite endearment, Italian for "brook" but he could just as easily call her any other affectionate nicknames he'd used in the past. He had plenty. She shot him a grateful smile.

Brigit was upon them in seconds. "What happened?"

"Tea, bring tea *pronto!*" Enrico commanded.

"Please," added Felix.

"Immediatamente." The housekeeper scurried down the hall, her slippers slapping on the tiles.

"Into the salon and onto the chaise longue you go." Felix was steering her into the long white mural-painted gallery salon as if she were an aging dowager. He paused before an antique daybed upholstered in white velvet—white velvet!—and urged her to sit.

"Felix, no! I'm filthy," she pointed out. "Let me clean myself up first and I'll meet you back here in fifteen minutes."

Enrico and Felix exchanged glances.

"It's all right," she assured them. "Everything's quiet inside me at the moment. It's safe enough." Or so she hoped but what did she know? She hadn't expected to be attacking people on the streets of Florence, either. Her dreams must have triggered something. She sensed that Gabriela would soon experience her first of many traumas.

"Should I wait outside your door?" Felix asked.

"No." She patted his arm. "I'll be fine."

Minutes later she was back inside her guest suite, keeping her eyes averted from the tapestries and Felix's beloved antiques. With luck the present would remain fixed.

Quickly, she washed her face and sponged down every cut and scrape before climbing into her jeans and sweater. Unlike her friends, she couldn't dress herself in the most luxurious fabrics, though she had such a longing for them sometimes it was almost painful. She still kept scraps of silks and velvets in her apartment back home for the sole purpose of rubbing them as if they were worry stones. Any textile could be a trigger these days so she was more careful.

Back in the salon, she waited alone for her friends to join her. Perhaps she was once again burdening their friendship. For all the years she'd known them, it had always been the same. They were like the brothers she'd never had, two guys who had rescued her long ago without realizing what a stew they'd waded into.

She had been the young Canadian fledgling designer on a work term with the famed maestro Mario Barone and they had been the underlings who would later launch a top design house of their own. Mario had commended all three for their creative brilliance and hard work, but only she had crashed and burned while her friends went on to reach their potential. Sometimes her losses piled upon her so heavily she couldn't bear it. She stared at the painted wall, wishing she could just dive right into the scene and hide out even though she knew there was no safe place for her anymore.

When the men joined her minutes later bearing a tray of tea, she smiled brightly. "I see you redecorated the salon again. When I came for Mario's funeral, it was very minimalist, if I recall."

"Felix thought it too boring, like being in a priest's cell, he said. Imagine," Enrico told her, placing the tray on the marble table before taking a seat in the wing chair with his ankles crossed. Still in his silk pjs. "It was his turn to lead the decoration squad this time while I merely backed away and allowed him to proceed."

"It's a beautiful, restful room," Brooke said, gazing at velvet furnishings. Also fabulous, luxurious, and totally impractical. "I could just lose myself here."

"And everything else besides. Busy, busy, busy." Enrico rolled his eyes.

"And Rico thinks it too much like a movie setting," Felix said with a sigh.

"I never say such things."

"Did you two paint the mural yourselves?" she asked. Stalling, really.

The mural stretched the entire length of the room and was like an invitation to another world. Soft Arcadian green, trees and foliage fringing a meandering blue river with white temples on hills, satyrs chasing nymphs—no wait: satyrs chasing satyrs—and birds flitting in the sky...

"My doing," Felix acknowledged. "Rico wouldn't touch it."

"Are you ready to begin?" Enrico prompted.

She studied them. Yes, they had aged some since she'd last seen them but not by much. Nearly the same height, both dressed in different pieces of their winter men's sleepwear collection, they made a picture of male sartorial splendor, Italian style. Felix was balding with a soft, kind face while Enrico was darkly handsome, a beautiful man for whom she once had a crush before realizing he didn't share the attraction. Both were immensely talented and endlessly patient and she was like the foundling sibling that periodically wreaked havoc on their lives.

"I am." She had to get this over with. Either that or resign herself to living a fractured life.

"Permit me to assist. When last we heard—" Enrico cleared his throat "—you were under a doctor's care in Toronto and making headway with the medication. You said that there had been some progress made, perhaps a diagnosis?"

"Schizophrenia," she began. "Of course they thought that. How else do you explain the hallucinations?"

"Yes, how do you?" he asked in that tone she knew so well.

She hurried on. "They believed me to be mentally ill, of course, and I accepted that at first, but as I studied further, I began to realize that the explanation was not so tidy, after all. The mind is like another frontier only partially understood, and as long as we approach it solely in scientific terms, it will remain that way."

"The mind is indeed a tangled thing," Felix acknowledged. "There is no shame, no need to be embarrassed. Mental illness is not a scourge." He shot her one of his brilliant smiles.

"Yes, mysteries exist there that we don't even begin to understand, especially if we continue to approach it with science alone. Despite evidence to the contrary, I am not mentally ill, at least not by current definitions."

"And yet you run about in the streets attacking carabinieri," Enrico remarked, his sharply angled face fierce in the lamplight, "and speak to people not there."

"Not there in this century but they existed once," she began, "approximately five hundred years ago, more or less." Their shocked expressions were expected. "After much research and testing, the details of which I can explain at a later time, I began to realize that I was acting out the life of another but not sequentially, which just makes it more challenging." She paused to take a deep breath. "But before I tell you anything about her or describe what I've pieced together so far, please understand that even mentioning her name could pitch me back into her life. I have no idea what triggers these episodes except to say that I expect them to become more frequent, more intense, now that I am back in Florence. I—"

"Are you saying that you're are experiencing some sort of past life regression?" Felix exclaimed, slapping a hand to his heart. "Oh, my God, Ruscello, really! That explains everything, doesn't it, Enrico?"

Enrico shot him a sharp glance. "Yes, if we believed such things, which I can't say I do." He leaned forward. "Admittedly, it would make a neat explanation for your behavior. Do you remember the time you were begging Felix not to continue a relationship with me in case he'd be flogged in the streets or worse, all in some old Italian dialect that we had to call in an expert to decipher?" His features had hardened.

Oh, my God. She had forgotten that. She stared at her friend. "That was spoken Italian in the mid-fifteenth century but it wasn't me talking but her and I'm guessing she was attempting to be helpful. Homosexuality was being explored by the humanists in Renaissance Florence but the church was still punishing any they caught in the act. You know all that, of course."

"Of course," he said dryly, "and I think any sentient being who knows a little history knows this, also."

"Look, Enrico, Felix, bear with me. I can prove my hypothesis with a little time and a lot of patience on your part and more besides. I need to tell you about what's happening to me."

"Such as?" Enrico asked.

"On some days, I can describe in detail scenes I couldn't possibly have experienced and tell you things there's no way I—or anybody in this century, for that matter—could know. I've booked three weeks off work for the sole purpose of getting to the bottom of this once and for all—and seeing you both, of course. This is do or die for me now. It began here and now here it must end."

"And what job is that you've taken leave from? The last we heard you could not keep employment or a relationship, either," Enrico said.

"Do not be unkind, Rico," Felix warned.

Brooke twisted her hands in her lap. "It's all right. I deserve the tone and will answer anything. I'm currently working at a graphic design company as a receptionist. It's as close as I can get to the design field without spinning off my rocker. As for relationships..." She shrugged. "No man can stand my behavior for long. Can you blame them? The last guy walked out on me when I started screaming the name Jacopo. His name was Fred, by the way."

Enrico and Felix exchanged glances again.

"I know, deranged by any other name and yet I am not crazy," Brooke insisted. "But I swear I'll see this to the end and claw my life back."

"And we will do everything we can to assist you, won't we, Enrico?" Felix turned to his partner, who was already on his feet pacing the room.

"And what do the doctors say of this notion of yours?" Enrico turned to stare at her from where he stood mid-salon.

"It's not 'a notion,' Enrico. It's my diagnosis of a compounding situation that doesn't bear any other explanation. Even the doctors agree that schizophrenia, psychosis—you name it—doesn't behave like my affliction. Maybe multiple personalities comes closer but even that doesn't work. Nothing explains why I only experience these fractures when attempting something creative or visiting a museum, seeing a piece of Renaissance art, or am anywhere in my beloved Florence. Nothing explains why I sometimes speak Latin, a language I don't know in depth, and can quote whole tracks of ancient manuscripts at times but seem lost at others, or why I remember things I couldn't possibly know in excruciating detail."

"But didn't you tell us that you had studied Latin in school?" Enrico demanded, taking a step toward her.

She met his eyes. "One year in grade ten and half of grade eleven before I had to drop out...because I was getting headaches." She had forgotten that, too. Nobody had believed her then, either. The school counselor had kept lecturing her on how someday she might be glad to know the ancient language. "I am not mentally ill," she said with more asperity than she intended. "I'm living another's life and desperately need to regain my own. Please believe and help me. You've always been such good friends," she whispered. "Even twenty years ago when my world shattered in this very city, you were there to help me pick up the pieces."

"And perhaps you are missing a few still, yes?" Enrico said under his breath.

Felix shot him a quick, angry glance. "Of course we'll help you, Ruscello. Pay no attention to Enrico. He has not been himself lately."

But Brooke was on her feet now, gazing around, whispering, "Where is this place, Father?"

3

*G*abriela blinked, trying to remove the blurriness that smeared her vision. What was wrong with her? Why was everything shifting and moving in and out of focus again? This was her house, her street, and yet the house didn't look quite still or quite right but the need to get inside overwhelmed her. And where had Father gone? Had they taken him? She could not even remember how she got there.

Banging on the door, she called out until at last Maria, the maid, appeared. Why was the inner bolt thrown?

"Gabriela, where were you?" asked the girl, not much older than Gabriela but a good worker, though hopeless in many ways. Her mother had taken her in after she had lost both parents and the girl always tried her very best but at times could be so infuriating. "Your father has been waiting for you and your mother has been calling out. Did you not bring the midwife?"

"Midwife?"

The girl stood before her twisting her apron in her hands, small, pale-skinned, her hair caught up in a head scarf. She loved to chastise Gabriela if she could get away with it. "Are you truly not right in the head? I hear your parents saying that you behave so strangely and see that it is so. You left two gongs ago to fetch Signora Asti and here you return home alone."

Father appeared in the hall behind them, the grooves beneath his eyes like gouges in the candlelight. "Maria, go warm a posset for your mistress and be quick about it," he said, sending the girl scurrying down the hall.

"Father? How did you get home before me?" He had already changed his tunic and the gnash on his temple looked all but healed. "What did they do to you? I looked for you everywhere. They took me to this place that I cannot describe, like nothing I've ever seen. I—"

He grabbed her shoulders and gave her a little shake. "Gabriela, stop this. We have not the time for your confusions. You must know that your mother is very ill. The baby struggles to be born. Did Signora Asti refuse to come? She promised she would tend your mother no matter how dangerous the streets but I should have known that she might forsake us."

"Signora Asti? But, Father, we were just together in the piazza and were set upon by ruffians and now you ask about the midwife? Has Mama taken a turn so quickly?"

"That was weeks ago. Gabriela, what is amiss with you? I need you to pull yourself together and help me now." He appeared so stern but she could sense the fear that ruled him now.

Gabriela was about to protest when her mother cried out from the floor above. "Mama!"

Bunching her dress in her hands, she ran upstairs and down the hall to where her mother lay in the grand bed father had purchased only the year before, the Celebration bed, he had called it, though Gabriela had found little to celebrate since its arrival.

She could not bear to look and yet she couldn't tear her gaze away. Her mother lay on her back, her usually ruddy complexion bleached pale, her eyes searching the room as if seeking something to cling to. Red stained the sheets...a bitter color drenched in pain. *Not again, please, God, not again...*

"Gabriela, at last. My dear child, come to me." Her mother lifted a weak hand.

"But, Mama, I must fetch the midwife. I tried earlier—" She hesitated. But had she? Yes, but the door had been barricaded. "But I could not...find her. I will find another."

"No, wait. Please, Gabriela." Her mother struggled to sit, her dark hair coiling in damp strands around her neck. "It is too late," she whispered. "The baby is gone. I was only meant to have one child. I know that now... God punishes us...for striving to be what we are not...and for making rich things...for people...when we are meant to...walk the path of humility."

"Lucinda, my love, that is not true," protested her father, entering the room. "We prosper! God wishes us to succeed and so we have done by hard work in His name."

"Not in His name," she cried, "in the Medici name! The good Lord wishes us to tread in Jesus's footsteps and instead we fashion riches for the grand...to make them appear grander still. It is a sin...and now we are being punished! Another babe lost this night!"

"Do not waste your breath, Mama," Gabriela pleaded, while gently lowering her mother back on the pillows. "You must rest while I find one who will help the babe to be born."

"The babe is gone, Gabriela. Look at the blood. As before. It was a miracle that you were born but that was back when we were poor still."

"Hush, Mama. If Signora Asti will not come, I will find another."

Now she remembered how all of Florence's citizens hid behind their doors this night. Cowards all. Unrest still brewed in the streets and many refused to poke their heads out after dark but soon the sun would dawn on Easter Sunday and the faithful would attend mass. Surely none would dare attack good citizens of the republic on such a holy day? She would find a midwife and demand that they attend her mother in the name of the Lord but it was best to get a good start.

"Mama, you rest now. I will find help."

Her father placed a hand on her shoulder. "No, Gabriela. I will go, as was my intention before you insisted that you knew the quickest routes. This is no task for a girl."

"But it is the perfect task for a girl, Father. No one will pay me any mind and I do know quickest routes and the best ones, too," she said as she squeezed her mother's limp fingers before pulling her cloak closer about her shoulders. "It is the way of children and women to seek out the safest paths through the most dangerous streets and I have had much practice delivering things every way which. Stay with Mama. If you step out, they will attack you whereas I can go about unnoticed." That is why she went on foot so as to not attract attention while her father refused to leave home without Francesca, his mare.

Father argued all the way down the stairs but Gabriela knew she was right and that gave her strength. "Stay with Mama," she implored him. "You know the rabble awaits anyone they know to be Medici supporters whereas I am but a girl hardly worth notice. I will return within the hour."

"Take Chiara to make good speed," her father called as she made for the door.

"No, to go on foot is by far the safest way." And with that she flung open the door and plunged into the night.

Their street remained thick with shadows, the houses tucked safe behind high stone walls. The citizens of Florence constantly feared attack from thieves and enemies so houses were like fortresses, theirs being no different, though humbler than many. Like the others, they housed the stables on the first level across a tiny courtyard with the living area on the floors above. Their neighborhood was a mix of rich and poor—poorer the closer to the river where the tanneries huddled and richer down the road toward the church where they had their home, as well as others like the painter Alessandro di Mariano di Vanni Filipepi, or Sandro, as her father called him.

Most did not burn torches this early in the morning, it being only a few hours before dawn, yet far down the street past their neighborhood church, the Chiesa di San Salvadore di Ognissante, which they called simply the Ognissante, still shone brightly. As it should.

Farther down still, the Palazzo Vespucci burned a torch in every bracket, too. Gabriela hesitated. Might there be a physician living there now? She had heard such a rumor and had encountered the old man Master Vespucci had called to tend his wife many times while she was fitting the failing beauty.

The Lady Simonetta was indeed as lovely as claimed, though Gabriela had watched her decline with the wasting illness over the months. Pressing herself deeper into the shadows, she wondered if she should risk pounding on their door and asking for assistance? Master Vespucci knew her. Would he refuse? Certainly the Lady Simonetta would help, for she was as kind as she was beautiful, but perhaps now too weak. She took a step forward but stopped. Voices coming from ahead sent her pressing back into the shadows.

"We cannot attack the Vespuccis!" a man said in a harsh whisper. "We have been told to stir unrest after mass and nothing more."

"For another florin I will gladly tear the Medici and all their friends from limb to limb so that the true rulers, the Pazzis, rise to power. These scum prosper from Medici coffers! Look at that artist Botticelli, who lives just yonder. Let us be at them and bang down their doors!"

"Imbecile!" another man growled. "We will be slaughtered by the guards if you attack the Vespucci, for we are only two. The others await. Besides, our instructions are clear: Riario says we go to the piazzas after mass and call for all to rise up against the tyrants. We are to stir an uprising, not kill Florentine citizens!"

"But one will help the other, surely?"

The voices faded as the men continued on their path, leaving Gabriela to stand fixed to the spot. *They were to rise up against the Medici today of all days, Easter Sunday?* She must warn them, warn somebody, perhaps alert her father, but what could he do? He would not venture out until mass and maybe not even then, not with Mama and the unborn baby.

No, if anything were to be done, it had to be by her. As Mama said, the baby was already gone and Gabriela would send a physician to attend her mother as soon as she found one, but she must first warn the Medici.

That decided, she left her hiding place and continued on behind the men, keeping close to the thick shadows that clotted against the walls, slipping from pillar to post as if a shadow herself. By the route they took down the narrow streets toward the city center, she guessed they were heading toward the Piazza della Signoria. That's where she would go if wanting to incite mischief and it was but a short distance from there to the Palazzo Medici. And she knew of a shortcut.

But the way was still long and sometimes the men stopped to talk with others, sending Gabriela scurrying into doorways or to duck behind carts. Many times Father and she had gone this way but always on their mounts and usually in daylight. It surprised her how different everything seemed in the dark, easier to slink about, for sure, but stranger, too. She must stay alert to every dark pocket in case another hid there.

Every shutter remained closed, every door shut, yet ahead the clop of hoofbeats told her that many roamed this morning and not just the conspir-acists she followed. Though she remained a good distance behind, it seemed as though the men were gathering in numbers.

But suddenly she was shaking and the world around her seemed to break into fragments like a mirror tossed to the ground...

4

"Father!"

"Stop calling me that!"

A man was shaking her, shaking her until her eyeballs rattled. She shoved him away. "Why are you here and not with Mama? They will attack you! They mean to rise up against the Medici this morn and kill them, both brothers! We must warn them!"

"Oh, my God, preserve me," the man muttered, turning away.

Gabriela stared as his face flickered from her father's to another man's as if etched glass overlayed one upon the other. "Enrico?" she whispered. Why did she know this man?

"At last, Felix, she recognizes me!" he cried, turning to the other who standing by.

Brooke pressed her hands to her face, trying to rein in the panic galloping in her chest. It wasn't her panic, she reminded herself, but it may as well have been. "Shit! It's happening again." She dropped her hands. "Don't you see? Gabriela is about to witness the Pazzi conspiracy as it played out hundreds of years ago! She'll take me with her and there's no way I can stop it!"

Enrico swore in two languages. "The Pazzi conspiracy now! I cannot take this anymore," he said, and strode down the hall. They were near the elevator but Brooke had no recollection of how she got there.

"Wait, Rico," called Felix, one arm holding Brooke close. "Please, love, Stephani said she will be up directly."

Brooke turned to him. "Not Dr. Stephani Marino?"

"*Sì*, the Renaissance scholar, now retired. You met her once when she confirmed that you were speaking an old Italian dialect, remember? She now owns the flat below."

"The one who told you she thought me a particularly brilliant kind of fraud?" Brooke asked, aghast. The thought of being scrutinized by that sharp-eyed academic brought her as about much comfort as a pending root canal.

"Ah, Ruscello, I know you two did not hit it off at first but she is an expert and has changed her mind regarding your affliction. She has even become a friend now that she is retired. She often asks about you and seems more than eager to assist. When I called a few minutes ago, she promised to come immediately."

"Oh, joy," Brooke whispered.

As if on cue, the elevator door bell rang. Enrico leaned forward on one leg with a dancer's grace and buzzed her up. "It is only for Steph's sake that I remain," he said. "I admit that my patience wears thin."

"Do you think I want my life to collide with another's, Rico? I'm trying to escape this madness," Brooke cried.

Before he could answer, the doors slid open and out stepped Dr. Stephani Marino, a bit disheveled in a gray tracksuit—probably cashmere—with a burgundy sweater tossed over her shoulders and feet shoved into a well-worn pair of furry mules. Not quite the elegant woman Brooke remembered but her face remained just as lean, the dark eyes just as haunted, and those cheekbones below the prominent aquiline nose just as sharp. A great deal more gray streaked the straight shoulder-length dark hair than Brooke remembered but then she must be at least sixty now.

"If you say one insulting word to me, one of us will walk straight down that elevator and it won't be me," Brooke told her.

The woman's shocked expression was almost comical. But then she grinned. "Signorina, I forget how booed you are." The woman nodded. "How happy I am that we meet again, too." She was speaking English with careful and perfect enunciation in that deep, smoky voice of hers. "Forgive me for my behavior at our last meeting. I hope to be of more assistance than previously."

Last time they had met in an empty classroom and the professor clearly couldn't spare her the time. Brooke clenched her teeth at the memory.

Taking a step forward, the woman smiled at Enrico and Felix in turn before fixing her full attention on Brooke. "I was perhaps too abrupt all those years ago as a result of my then-ignorance but I ask that you forgive me and allow me to make this up to you. I have learned much since. In fact, your story fascinates me so that I pester the boys at every opportunity as to how you are getting along."

She referred to Enrico and Felix as "boys"? It seemed such a strangely Americanized, not to mention affectionate, term for her two friends. She shot each a quick look to see how they were wearing the term but neither seemed to mind. The friendship among the three must have deepened.

"That surprises me," Brooke told her. "I don't have a positive memory of your last encounter, Signora Marino."

"Please, call me Stephani as my friends do. You and I must become friends, you see."

"Seriously? Didn't you call me a 'deluded, overdramatic, attention-seeking psychopath,' Stephani?"

"Ah." She threw up her long hands. "You remember every word, proof that my careless proclamation was cutting as well as wrong, yes? How unkind of me. And opinionated. You are none of those things, of that I am convinced. In fact, you may just be one of the most incredible windows to another century alive today—a miracle of sorts—and I sincerely request another opportunity to assist you on the journey. I ask again, Signorina Carter, am I forgiven?"

"But what changed your mind?" Brooke asked, a little breathless. She could never forget that day when Felix took her to the Università degli Studi di Firenze to meet this severe woman, who had regarded her with such distain. Here, it seemed, stood an entirely different version.

Marino's full lips curved into a smile, quite a lovely one, in fact. In an instant she was ageless. "Very simple: during one of your 'events,' you quoted a few lines you claimed to be from an ancient Greek manuscript that I thought did not exist. Several years later, I learn from a colleague that such a manuscript does exist but remains in a private collection believed to have once belonged to Lorenzo de' Medici but was never in the public domain. How could that not demand my attention? There is no way you could have known this since it was not discovered until very recently—another valuable tome buried alive in a private collection. After further research, which we can discuss later, I knew that you, Signorina Carter, are walking through time. May I call you Brooke?

"Call me anything you want except delusional."

Stephani let out a bark of laughter. "Oh, this one is funny, yes? I like her." Striding up to Brooke, she tucked her hand into the crook of her arm, giving Brooke a moment to study the fabric of the tracksuit—cashmere, as expected. "Excellent. Now, tell me, Brooke, where is it you have just been this time?"

"She claims that she was on her way to the Pazzi conspiracy," Enrico muttered, striding behind them as Stephani steered her back to the salon.

"The Pazzi conspiracy!" The woman's face lit up as if they had mentioned a Christmas festival. "You are about to witness history, then?"

"I'd rather just get my life back," Brooke said. "I've known this particular event lies ahead in Gabriela's future but I really don't want to go there. Once I thought that being a sightseer in a famous historic moment might be an amazing experience but now realize that history comes with bolts of nightmare-inducing terror."

"It does!" Stephani agreed, squeezing Brooke's arm. "That is because you are recalling a life lived amid much upheaval. Often the simpler lives slip into the fabric of the soul's memory unseen, sì?"

"You are talking reincarnation," Brooke said.

"Are not you?" the woman asked, fixing her with her inscrutable gaze.

"I am. I'm just so relieved to find that someone else accepts it so readily."

"It is because of you that I accept it. You have sent me on a journey of my own for which I am changed forever. Your experiences and mine are not as far removed as you may think." Turning, she said over her shoulder: "We need a drink, boys. What do you say to vermouth or maybe a touch of scotch?"

"I say it's four o'clock in the morning, Stephani darling. Maybe a touch of caffeine would be more appropriate?" That was Felix. "Should I get the cappuccino going?"

"So dull, these two," sighed Stephani. "I believe alcohol is a fine accompaniment any hour of the day, but if you must, bring the caffeine." Turning to Brooke, she added: "Now, let us sit and discuss all that has happened to you, from the beginning, yes?"

"The beginning is a very long story since this has been going on for over a decade." She may as well tell Stephani the short version. It was as if the woman was pulling her into her orbit as surely as had Gabriela. "At first these feelings would wash over me, feelings that appeared to come from nowhere and had nothing to do with anything I was experiencing at the time. That was when I opted for psychiatric help, though all the meds they prescribed only numbed my emotions without eliminating them."

"Yes, modern science is not prepared for these situations."

They sat side by side on the cushy white velvet couch while Stephani pulled out a packet of cigarettes from her side pocket. Brooke watched in amusement as the former professor attempted to light one on the sly by shielding her actions from Enrico's watchful eye.

"Absolutely not!" Enrico glared. "Put those noxious things away. Smoke on the balcony, if you must," he said in Italian, adding a couple of spicy expletives.

Stephani threw up her hands. "How tedious you can be, Rico! Health is very overrated if one cannot enjoy their vices. Very well. Dear Brooke, please continue. How and when did your experiences intensify?" She slipped the cigarettes back into her pocket. "When I saw you last you seemed to be falling into snippets, pieces of conversations, and events."

"Over the years," Brooke began slowly, "they became accompanied by what I thought were hallucinations—people appearing before my eyes whom I knew couldn't be there, vividly and in excruciating detail. Then, in the past year, I'd suddenly be catapulted into another space and time. It felt—*feels*—like I'm falling into a big-screen movie, tangled in somebody else's plot, saying their lines, being carried along against my will trapped in another's body. And there's no reliable sequence, either. I relive some scenes more than once. Sometimes I'm plunged into an action as an adult and sometimes as a child often in disconnected flashbacks, but I always have a sense that there's something significant looming ahead."

Stephani grimaced. "Yes, that is the way."

Enrico muttered under his breath.

Stephani turned to him. "Have you had no such experiences, Enrico, really —no déjà vu, no conviction that this is only the most recent of your lives? Do you not think these things?"

"I'm getting a headache, that's what I think. Let me see how Felix is getting along with our cappuccinos. Brooke, don't go anywhere." And with that he leaped to his feet and slipped from the room.

"I'm afraid our friend is not going to easily accept what's happening to you, Brooke," Stephani remarked, turning to her. "He has always been the most resistant of the pair."

Brooke grinned. "Which is why I'm holding off telling him he was my daddy in another life."

Stephani threw back her head in a throaty laugh. "Yes, do wait to announce that. However, perhaps before your story is complete, he will come to understand. We are all connected, you know."

"I do know. At times I see two faces in an overlay and sometimes even three. So far, I've identified far fewer than I anticipated—I expected to recognize Felix, for instance—but I'm thinking that maybe I have yet to meet him in Gabriela's life."

"Possibly. They may also be souls that prefer to hide themselves across the centuries, sentient souls who realize that they live over and over again."

29

"Sentient souls? Is there really such a thing?" She rubbed a hand across her face. "Uh-oh. Things are beginning to shift. Damn it! I really want to stay present for much longer." Brooke fixed on her Stephani as if she were an anchor holding her in place but she could barely hear her words, let alone see her face. The cappuccino machine whirred far down the hall.

"Does time waver for you already?" Stephani asked.

"Yes." Brooke gazed about hoping to find something so resolutely modern that it might help fix her to this century. "Sometimes it hits with no warning and now that I'm in Florence the phenomena are occurring more frequently. I'm trying desperately to stay present because I don't want to witness the Pazzi conspiracy. I have a feeling it's a trauma point for Gabriela. Maybe if I can stare at something ultramodern." But this was the wrong kind of decor for what she needed—all antiques and old-world charm.

"Maybe coffee will help. The boys should return in a moment. Is she aware of your presence?" she heard Stephani ask as Brooke's gaze landed on Felix's iPhone on the table. Maybe that would keep her anchored.

"Do you mean Gabriela? I don't think so."

"Gabriela...yes. Do not be startled if you find that you may be able to communicate with her at some point."

"Really?" Brooke shook her head as if to shake away her blurring vision.

Stephani leaned forward. "Would it surprise you to know that what you are experiencing has a name?"

"Lucid reincarnation. Yes, I've been researching, too," Brooke replied, thinking that it was best if she kept on talking. Events dragged her into the past, not conversations.

"Lucid reincarnation," Enrico repeated, slipping into the room with a tray of coffee mugs, Felix following holding two carafes. "A most officious and convincing title, if one believes in reincarnation. Sounds almost Californian."

"Whether or not you believe in something does not mean it does not exist, my dear," Felix said under his breath as he slid a big cup of cappuccino on the coffee table beside Brooke and beamed her an encouraging smile. "Warm milk? Café?"

Shaking her head, she reached for the cup and sipped the rich foamy brew with pleasure. Caffeine helped everything.

"I am a good Catholic boy," Enrico said with a shrug.

"You are neither good nor Catholic, dearest," Felix countered. "You have not been to church for years, ever since you had that argument with that priest, in fact."

"Nonsense," protested Enrico. "Our 2019 collection was held in the Chiesa di Santa Maria in Siena."

"Deconsecrated and now a museum, as you know," his partner said, taking a seat opposite Stephani and Brooke. "It just happened to be ideal for our stained-glass collection."

"I loved that line," Brooke said quietly, relieved that the world around her had begun to settle again. "I'd hoped to base a collection on glass references long ago."

"And we dedicated that collection to you for that very reason," Enrico reminded her, "and sent you several pieces."

"Which I've brought with me." She smiled, briefly feeling that tingle of excitement that textiles, pattern, and ideas once conjured, feelings she'd since stifled in case they triggered an event. Those rich silks and velvets carefully wrapped in her suitcase were a case in point: she dared not wear them and yet could not leave them behind. She squeezed her eyes closed. Thinking of textiles often lured her into Gabriela's life. She needed to remain grounded.

"Tell us more about Gabriela, Brooke, unless you think that an unwise thing to do at the moment." Stephani reached for her cup. "Where does she fit into this extraordinary period of time you are glimpsing?"

"Not glimpsing, *living*," Brooke said, her eyes still closed. She brought the coffee to her lips and sipped deeply. "She's a seamstress and so far I've only experienced her life up to her early teens. Just once for a few minutes, I breathed her in the skin of a much older woman so I know she lived well into adulthood."

"A seamstress!" That was Felix. "Oh, how fitting! There, I just made a pun in English. I am so proud. Is that why her soul has followed you here?"

"Maybe," Brooke acknowledged.

"But how did this seamstress learn Latin and tracts of Roman and Greek manuscripts?" Enrico demanded. "That is hardly common for a woman of lowly birth."

A sudden vision of an extraordinary library flooded Brooke's mind with such clarity that she almost gasped, though still she could feel the couch beneath her. "Because she was educated by Lorenzo de' Medici's children's tutor. Oh, my God! How do I know that? Her father, tailor to the Medici, seems to have become a member of Lorenzo de' Medici's extended circle of artists and scholars. Through Lorenzo, Gabriela learned Latin and Greek. I mean, I know that is true but not how I know it." She turned to Stephani. "How would the daughter of a tailor be permitted such an education?"

Stephani held her gaze. "Because she must have been an extraordinary girl who became an equally extraordinary woman."

Brooke set her mug down with trembling hands and stood up. "She was."

"Brooke, darling, are you all right?"

She blinked into Felix's concerned face. "I'm seeing things…"

"No, not now!" Stephani cried. "Boys, we must get her something to eat, keep her blood sugar up."

"Brigit is up and will make breakfast," Brooke heard Enrico say. For God's sake, can't we keep her with us?"

But the world was shifting before Brooke's eyes, not, she realized with relief, into cobbled streets but merging into the interior of a palazzo. "I think I'm going back…to the Medicis…"

* * *

"Gabriela!" She saw her father rise from his seat, sensing that he was warning her with his gaze, yet all she could do was stare around the room, unable to tear her eyes away. Never had she seen such a place, did not know that such existed. Painted blue ceiling, stars between images of birds and flowers above, books on shelves everywhere—and such books! Her father did not have near so many and not a single one encrusted with gold and jewels like these.

"Are they books or are they treasures?" she whispered.

"Are not they one and the same, Gabriela? Come, show the maestro and your father how far you have progressed," the man named Poliziano, her part-time tutor, said behind her.

One such book lay open on a slanted shelf nearby, its pages displaying a vibrant scene of people working in a field with a white castle in the background and figures painted along the margins in colored inks with gold leaves curling all about. The same starry blue as the ceiling rose above the workers on the page, a blue like she had rarely seen because she knew it to be so precious—lapis lazuli, a pigment as holy as the Virgin's robes—but here it covered the sky!

"Do you know what that is, Gabriela?"

She tore her eyes away. A man stood before her, a man with a dusky voice and straight brown hair, his nose seemingly pushed into his face as if from a wall or perhaps even a fist. Dark sparkling eyes and wide lips spread into a smile, an unattractive face but one which she found strangely appealing, even more so as she came to know him.

"A book, my lord," she said, gazing up at him. Rich red tunic with five tiny buttons at the neck—her father's tailoring in the finest Venetian red dyed wool. The great Lorenzo de' Medici, the Magnifico, the master of the house, of Florence itself. She should bow, lower her gaze, something, but she never did and he never seemed to mind.

"Yes, it is a book, a French Book of Hours," he said. "A devotional book that contains the calendar of church feasts, psalms, and much more. That one is a particularly exquisite example and the page you see lies open onto a psalm. Show us how you can read Latin, Gabriela."

Her name on his tongue sent a flush climbing her cheeks. "Yes, sir." She stole a glance toward her father, who stood as if he'd been caught smuggling sweets from her mother's pantry. He'd always seemed so uncomfortable that his daughter learned along with the Medici children.

"Read a few lines, then. Begin anywhere," the great Lorenzo de' Medici told her, pointing to the book, "but do not touch the pages."

Stepping up to the slanted shelf, her hands behind her back, she read the first words she saw, scripted as they were in a heavy dark pointed hand. Latin had always sounded meaty on her tongue, as if she needed to chew carefully to swallow even a mouthful: *"Veneruntque duo angels Solomam vespers sedate Loth in forbids civitas qui vidisset suurexut et ivies obviate is adoravitgue in terra."* Strong sounding, like Roman soldiers marching into the distance.

"Excellent. Now translate into the common tongue," the Magnificent commanded.

She wet her lips and began in Italian. "And the two angels came to Sodom in the evening, and Lot was sitting at the gate of the city." The actual text said something like *in* the gate but that made no sense so she substituted. "And seeing them, he rose up and went to meet them and dropped by falling on the ground." She turned toward the great Medici. "I think that means that he bows low before the angels, for why would he drop?"

The Magnificent stared at her briefly before throwing back his head and emitting his raspy laugh. Poliziano and her father himself joined in the mirth, leaving her at a loss. What had she said that was so humorous?

"You are quite right, Gabriela: Why would Lot 'drop'?" The Magnifico nodded, still smiling. "Come here so I may look at you."

Poliziano placed a hand on her shoulder and steered her into the center of the room. "Domenico, your girl is a prodigy of a student, intelligent enough not only to read but to comprehend what she is reading, as well."

"She is proceeding admirably," Magnifico said, nodding, "but sometimes I worry that as a tailor's daughter she is like to have little chance to use her skills once you marry her off."

33

"I fear that, too, my lord, and implore you to release her so that she may return soon to my roof."

"It would have been better had you had a son," Magnifico continued, gazing down at Gabriela with the tiniest of smiles. "Have you not often told us so?"

Her father, who had been standing still, shook his head. "And I pray that I may have one yet. It is true that I have opened my small library to Gabriela, too, while Poliziano tutors her—against her mother's wishes, I might add. She laps up the lot like a thirsty cat. Now that she reads Latin and Greek beyond the holy texts, what will become of her? She is a quick and able seamstress, clever in design as well as execution."

"Gabriela—" Poliziano turned his gaze to her "—are you to be a scholar and a seamstress, too?"

She lifted her chin. "Perhaps, sir. I do not see why one must exclude the other."

Her reply seemed to both surprise and please him. He clapped his hands. "Bravo, girl! May you lead the way out of the darkness that has besieged your sex!"

"Is she still betrothed?" the Magnifico asked her father.

"Indeed, my lord. Gabriela remains promised to my apprentice, Jacopo, who is but three years older. The lad has no interest in learning, it is true, but is good with the needle and sharp as a pin in tailoring. Together they will inherit my house, business, and contents, thus she will not be deprived."

"So you hope. And if you bear a son before then?"

"Then all this would change, of course, but I would trust that any son of mine would allow my house to run according to my wishes, which would include his sister and her family remaining under the roof. We do not have a huge house, my lord, but large enough."

"Indeed, let us hope this works out according to your plan for it would be a shame to douse such a light as I see burning in her eyes." The great man stepped up to Gabriela and gazed down. "The Lady Clarice and my mother, Lady Lucrezia, approve of your sewing, Gabriela di Domenico, and far prefer your attentions to any other. I, in turn, approve of your mind, which, to me, is at least as valuable, if not more so. You are always welcome in the House of Medici, as is your father."

"Thank you, my lord." And she dipped a bow, though in truth she knew her efforts to be without much grace.

"Now wait in the hall until your father and I have finished our business."

"Yes, sir." She turned toward the still-open door, stopping in her tracks at the sight of Bianca's murderous face coming around the corner.

"You! You wanton, disobedient girl! How dare you enter any room in this house unbidden." She snatched Gabriela's arm and gave it a vicious twist as she yanked her toward the hall.

"Stop that, Bianca!" commanded the Magnifico with a surprisingly deep and powerful voice. "You will leave Gabriela di Domenico alone, and should I hear that you have laid a hand on her again, you will answer to me."

5

"*B*rooke, talk to us."

Somehow she'd ended halfway across the room, one hand rubbing her right shoulder and the other pushing away at some invisible thing.

"What's happening this time?"

She gazed at the man standing before her who seemed both familiar yet not.

"Did you hear somebody yelling?" she whispered.

"Speak either Italian or English," he demanded crossly. "I can barely understand you."

"She asked if we heard yelling, Enrico," said the other man. "No, we did not. Come back to the couch, Brooke."

She felt an arm around her shoulders, steering her back to the seat where she had been sitting a long time ago, or so it seemed. At least she remembered that much. She recalled some strange fissure of voices breaking into her head —a woman whom she seemed to fear and three men, but not these men and not this woman. Memory flooded back. Clasping her hands in her lap, she let the words tumble out.

"I was just in the library of Lorenzo the Magnificent," she whispered. "I have clearly become a student with Lorenzo's children. I mean, *Gabriela* has— was—and she speaks Latin and some Greek, too. The scholar Poliziano as well as her father educated her. Amazing."

"Tell us what you saw," Felix urged.

"No, wait," the woman, Stephani, on the couch beside her cautioned. "It might induce another time walk."

"It's all right. This was just another flashback but nothing terrifying and a version of one I've had many times before. Just a group of us standing in the library. I was still a child or at least not much older than the last time I stepped into Gabriela's life. It can't have happened much before the Pazzi event."

Stephani squeezed her arm. "Be careful. Any reference you make to that event may pitch you back into the thick of it, something you must do eventually but not before you've had a chance to eat and rest."

Brooke gazed into the woman's dark eyes. "I think that event changes the course of Gabriela's life somehow," she whispered. "I must go through it with her so I can reach the other side."

"There is no other way to see Gabriela's life to the end." Stephani glanced up at the two men. "First we eat, permit Brooke to rest, and then we take off on a guided adventure, boys."

"You're joking," Enrico protested. "What in hell do you have in mind?"

"And how can you possibly come with me?" Brooke asked.

But before she could answer, Brigit announced breakfast and soon they were all sweeping into the breakfast room overlooking the spectacular view of old Florence with the spotlit Duomo, its iconic landmark, dominating the horizon. Brooke had almost forgotten how beautiful it all was. For a moment, all she could do was gaze at the band of rosy pink cracking the sky above the city.

"Dawn comes," she whispered. "I must be away and quickly."

"Here we go again," she heard someone say.

Swinging around, she scanned the street, trying to penetrate every shadow, every flicker of movement, but could see no one. Yet somebody followed her. Somebody had spoken. She could feel it with every fiber of her being. People with strange accents and even stranger clothes on her heels now. Turning away, she picked up her skirts and ran.

At first, she hardly cared which direction she went as long as it was the most direct route, the one that would bring her to the Medici palazzo fastest. Because it was Easter Sunday, she knew that the two Medici brothers would remain in the city rather than head for any one of their country villas. The Ladies Clarice and Lucrezia plus all of the children had been sent to the villa in the country for safety but why did she remember this now? That was as least as strange as the faces that appeared unbidden, faces that spoke to her in ways that seemed impossible.

Madness, demons? That's what the old priest had told her in confessional once. Possessed, he claimed. The demons must be burned out of her, he had cried in a tone that sent such fear into her heart that she fled the confessional box and hid for hours. To this day, she fervently hoped that he could not identify her since she'd had her hood drawn over her head but she guessed he knew. She was careful not to mention the voices to anyone ever since.

Briefly her steps faltered but soon she shook off her confusions and plunged on. All that mattered was that she warn the Medici, who now lay in danger.

The men she had been following before had disappeared but in their place other parties of men gathered on the street corners, some on horseback, some on foot, all of them whispering in low voices. Something was in the air, she could feel it. By the time she reached the Borgo Santi Apostoli, the sun had risen, turning the Duomo to gold in the distance, and the city that so often seemed filthy now lay adorned by that glowing orb. It must be a reminder from God that what she did, she did for Him. But the strange voices continued, too, asking her questions as if they rode upon her very shoulders. She shook them off, closed the door of her mind, and continued on.

People were now decking the churches with garlands of lilies, turning the air sweet with fragrance, while baskets of palm fronds awaited near the entrances for the ceremonies to begin. Merchants—and the city was full of them—hung lengths of wool and silk from their windows not only to fill the streets with color but to display their wares, which they did at every opportunity. Gabriela recognized the houses of many merchants where she and Father bought their fabrics, but today she slipped past unseen.

The day of Christ's resurrection was a jubilant feast day for the Florentines, one of the greatest of the year. All the citizens would attend mass decked in their finery and for once the men who regulated clothing excesses would not roam the streets waiting to pounce on the celebrators. But the glorious gowns her house had created for the Medici women and children would wait another day. Sad because the Lady Clarice did not want to leave any more than did her formidable mother-in-law, Lady Lucrezia, but the Magnifico knew it was too dangerous to permit them to stay.

And then as she strode down the narrow streets leading to the Piazza del Duomo, a sudden thought struck her with such force that it nearly knocked her sideways. She knew all at once what would happen that day, knew without a doubt that the youngest Medici brother would be murdered and beneath that very golden dome ahead! It was such a swift bolt of knowing that it arrived fully formed as if God Himself had placed it in her mind.

My Lord, no! It's me, Gabriela.

Panic ruled her now. She ran as if the devil himself were at her heels, snapping away with sharpened fangs as she leapt over baskets and pushed by carts, shoved through chatting citizens dressed in their finest, breaking into the Piazza del Duomo as the bells began to peal all over the city.

How could bells ring in jubilance on the feast of Christ's resurrection when a man would be murdered that very day? Could not everyone feel it, too? Why need she bear the truth alone? And how could she know that the Medicis would be ambushed and by one considered a friend?

Because I know it, you know it! You are not alone!

Of course, the brothers were well guarded. They knew the dangers with the Pazzi threat afoot, but never would they guess an atrocity would befall them on this of all days and inside the cathedral, too! That knowledge also whammed into Gabriela's mind with such force that she cried out. She must warn them.

How could Gabriela even get to the princes of the republic as they strode through the crowd heading to mass? She knew they must ride from the Piazza degli Uffizi through the streets to the Santa Maria del Fiore but there would be people everywhere, and guards besides. Who would listen to a girl screaming murder?

The crowd cheering "Maestro Medici" alerted her to their passage before she glimpsed them across the piazza, the two men riding toward the cathedral in their horses, their bold silk tunics gleaming in the morning sun, the horses livery glittering and their guards bearing the Medici trefoil standards high above. There they were! Cutting through the pressing crowd, she elbowed people aside, pushed away knots of children all dressed as bright as butterflies, crying out that she must get through.

"Wait, missy, what are you about?" cried one matron while another pinched her arm in passing, yet nothing slowed her pace.

"Do not go inside the cathedral!" she cried at the top of her voice over the sound of trumpets, cheers, and jeers alike. "They plan to ambush the Medici inside the church!"

"What nonsense is this?" said a man who clutched her by the hood of her cloak and yanked her backward. Holding her fast, he poked his face into hers and sneered. "What foolishness are you saying, girl?"

He was no friend of the Medici, she knew that much. "Nothing!" she spat. "Let me go. My brother awaits me." When still the man held on, she spun around and kneed him in the groin before scampering off across the piazza.

Lorenzo de' Medici had dismounted by now, leaving his horse with his man, and followed his brother up the steps toward the cathedral. Giuliano Medici, splendid in embossed yellow silk, chatted amiably to his friends, Bernardo Baroncelli and Francesco de' Pazzi, while Gabriela hurled toward them oblivious to the crowd, calling: "Beware the Pazzi murderers! Magnifico, it is I, Gabriela di Domenico, and I come to warn that they plan to kill you! It is an ambush!"

The great Lorenzo must have caught wind of her cries for he turned to gaze back over the crowd.

"It is me, Gabriela!" she called. "Beware the ambush!"

Magnifico frowned, peering into the crowd without catching sight of her until his companions urged him on. He turned and entered the cathedral. Gabriela may as well have been as invisible as a speck of mud on a shoe but she screamed her lungs out to no avail. They were gone.

What happened next was a flash of memories of people screaming, crying in shock and disgust, a body being carried out covered in bloodied yellow silk, while rumors whipped through the crowd: Lorenzo was dead; Giuliano was dead; the Pazzis now ruled Florence; the murderers must be found and hung!

Gabriela shoved her back against the cathedral as if its marble facade might somehow hold her together and watched, stunned, as men climbed on top of carriages to lecture how the Medici must be brought down. But the people didn't cheer as the plotters must have expected. Instead, shock blazed in their faces and sorrow burned in their eyes.

"Who defiles Easter Sunday?" they cried.

"What manner of men kills a man inside the glorious Santa Maria del Fiore?"

"To spill blood in the house of God is a crime against all that is holy and right."

"Why trade one tyrant for another?"

But then all the noise and clamor seemed to fade away like colors washed in sunlight and Gabriela found herself standing in the center of a large room on a thick rug with carved furniture all around and glowing paintings on the walls. Her father's hand pressed against her shoulder while the Magnifico sat in a chair, staring at her, sorrow grooving deep beneath his eyes and his arm in a silken sling.

"Tell me again how you knew of this Pazzi conspiracy." The great man's raspy voice had lost much of its power, worn down with weariness and grief.

"I—I don't know, my lord," she stammered. "The knowledge came to me all of a sudden like a bolt from the sky. I know not how else to explain it. Maybe the way in which the archangel Gabriel sent word to the Holy Mary that she would bear the Lord Jesus like I saw in the painting in the cathedral—like that."

"Blasphemy!" came a sharp whisper. She turned to see people standing in the shadows, at least five—three men, one of them a friar in a brown cassock, and two woman. The women she recognized at once, Lady Lucrezia and Lady Clarice, both veiled in black, but among the men, she only knew Master Poliziano.

Magnifico straightened in his seat to study Gabriela while she fought the urge to flinch. "You say that God told you that the Pazzi scum intended to kill my brother and I?"

"I do not know that it was God who sent the message, for why would God even allow such a travesty to happen on Easter Sunday and in His house? I only know that it hit me all at once like a beam to the brain and I knew that it was true so I had to warn you no matter what."

"My daughter did so despite the fact that her mama lay on her deathbed, my lord. Instead of fetching the midwife as she was told, she ran to warn you."

"I knew that the baby was already lost," she sobbed. "I did not think Mama was, too."

Her father squeezed her shoulder—hard. "To me that means she puts the Medici above all else. She's is loyal to you, my lord."

"She is possessed by the devil, more like it," said the priest, stepping forward. "Ask her what other voices she hears, my lord."

The Magnifico fixed Gabriela with his penetrating gaze, a gaze that seemed to hold her in their thrall, glittering with fierce intelligence, ruthless but not unkind. "Do you hear voices, Gabriela?"

She could not lie. "Sometimes, my lord," she said, wiping away her tears. Her dear mama. Had she hastened her death? "They seem to follow me and speak of things I cannot know. One I hear the most. She steps into my brain and I see faces, too. Not cruel, not evil, more like strange friends I never knew I had. One woman's voice always seems to go with me. I call her Voice."

"Demons!" croaked the priest. "She should be burned at the stake to expunge her sins!"

"Stop!" Magnifico held up his hand and the friar fell silent.

"My lord," spoke Lady Lucrezia from behind her black veil, her hands clasped before her. "She may have the Sight. Like the saints themselves, she witnesses revelations that are a gift from God."

"Or if I may suggest, my lord, that we test her in some manner," said the small dark man dressed in the blue velvet. "If, indeed, she knows what she cannot know and possesses the Sight as the Lady Medici suggests, then she should be able to answer a few simple questions. It could be that the girl over-heard the plotters on her way to the cathedral and that is how she received this supposedly divine foretelling."

It was all Gabriela could do to hold herself together by then. Her mama was dead, her father was hurt and angry, everyone looked at her as if she were a monster, and could it be true that she was? Did she forsake her own mother to warn the great Medici when nothing would change their destiny?

"Yes, good idea. Tell me, Gabriela, do you know the details of my brother's death?" asked Magnifico while his mama caught a sob in her throat, excused herself, and left the room, Lady Clarice following.

Once the women had left, Gabriela sought comfort somewhere, anywhere. The women's presence had been like a balm somehow—both mothers when she had just lost hers. By chance, her gaze landed on a painting of the Virgin Mary by an artist often seen about the Medici palazzo, the man her father called Sandro or "Botticelli." And it was such a beautiful painting, so rich in color and light, the Virgin's face loving yet strong. Mother Mary, too, had known much sorrow and Gabriela let her gaze rest there.

"Speak, girl," prompted the man in blue. "Tell us how the prince of men, our Giuliano de' Medici, died."

Did she know details of the Medici brother's death? No, of course not, only that he was pounced upon by men he believed to be friends and murdered right there in the cathedral, and yet her mouth opened as if with a will of its own.

"He received a fatal sword wound to the head and was stabbed nineteen times," she blurted as the words entered her head. *He died on the cathedral floor,* Voice told her. "And he died on the cathedral floor," Gabriela added before bursting into heaving sobs. Such aching sorrow filled her that she thought she might break in two.

The Magnifico jumped to his feet. "How could she know that? No one knows of this! My mother is right: the girl has the Sight. Had I heard her this morning, my brother might still be with us! I will allow nothing to harm her. Domenico, permit the girl to continue to be tutored here with my children under Master Poliziano. Pray allow her to be raised among my own children so I might keep watch on her special gifts."

Her father gripped both Gabriela's shoulders and pulled her back against him. "But, my lord, I am without wife. I cannot lose my daughter, too, I beg you! She works with me at my studio and her talents extend to the work we do. Though her behavior often addles me, she is all that I have left!"

Lord Magnifico ran a weary hand across his eyes. "Of course she is yours and we are all in mourning, yes? The pain of loss can crush us if we permit it. I ask this, then: allow Gabriela to come thrice weekly instead of once weekly until her sixteenth year. I will send other tailors to work in your studio to give you a hand while your extraordinary daughter benefits from my patronage and tutelage. I request that you allow this to happen, Domenico, for if Gabriela has the Sight, then she is not safe in the streets of Florence without protection."

"It must be kept secret, my lord," offered Poliziano.

"Indeed it must," Medici agreed, turning to the priest. "Father, I beseech you to say not a word."

The priest lowered his tonsured head but said nothing.

"Until her sixteenth year, then, after which she returns home. It is settled." She heard her father sigh. "My daughter, Gabriela, will come to this house on a regular basis under the guise of working as a seamstress for the ladies of your house, for I am sure you agree, my lord, that for her to go under any other reason would look amiss."

"Agreed," the great Medici nodded. "Now be away with you both so we may all bear our separate grief in private."

6

---

*B*rooke awoke in a soft bed with sunshine breaking through under the blinds on the opposite wall. The silhouette of her half-unpacked suitcase formed a little mountain on the luggage stand in front of the window and she recognized her shoes, kicked off on the fur rug at her feet.

The twenty-first century at last, she thought with relief as she rolled over onto her back to stare up at the ceiling. Thank God. The fifteenth century was wringing her out like a dishrag and leaving her limp and exhausted. At least she must have caught some sleep last night somehow.

Dragging her feet out from under the covers onto the rug, she sat for a moment trying to banish the sense of sorrow that filled her still, vestiges of Gabriela's life. Poor kid. They thought she could foretell the future and all because she, Brooke, rode inside her head with all her knowledge of what was to come. How could she shield the girl from her thoughts or should she even try? Maybe her sense of the future was supposed to somehow influence the past or already had? But then, even though Gabriela knew of the Pazzi conspiracy, nothing could stop the events from unfolding exactly as history had described. After all, the past was written in indelible ink, or so she hoped.

From somewhere in the flat, sounds of activity alerted her that it must be later than she thought—footsteps on the tiles, hushed voices, the clink of cups far down in the kitchen. Getting unsteadily to her feet, she strode to her suit-case and plucked out the first things her hands touched, her one cashmere

44

sweater in a brilliant shade of yellow and a pair of black velveteen jeans. May as well dress like she had more taste than money, which she desperately hoped to be true.

About twenty minutes later, she stood dressed, combing her curly brown hair before the bathroom mirror and thinking of ways to banish those dark circles under her eyes—concealer? She often wished that she could use one of those blur photo apps to removed unwanted lines. They worked like magic on her photos.

Leaving the bathroom, she strode across the room, opened her bedroom door, and stood breathing the scent of fresh-brewed coffee and something else. Linseed oil?

Turning, she watched the world around her fall away as her mind caught up with her eyes. Everywhere she looked, she saw paintings propped on easels in various states of completion, some merely drawings on wood or canvas, others fully formed masterpieces in glowing hues, all in a distinctive style she recognized at once. It was like being caught in a living, breathing gallery. She tried to suppress a gasp.

Curving, glowing, vibrant pictures so alive they nearly leapt from the canvas. One large piece straight before her displayed a scene of a goddess reclining in a field of flowers while cherubs attended her with loving attention—bringing bouquets of flowers, golden goblets clutched in their chubby fingers, all while her lover Mars waited nearby, seeming content just to gaze upon her loveliness with a lazy, satiated gleam in his eyes. Unfinished, yet powerful, it reminded Brooke of the Mars and Venus masterpiece or perhaps *Primavera*, but it was undoubtedly of the same period and created under the hand of the same master, Sandro Botticelli.

Oh, my God! Am I really here?

Something like a gasp escaped Brooke's throat, only she knew in an instant that it wasn't her throat but Gabriela's. "I haven't seen any of these before," the lips that weren't hers exclaimed. "I'm just so overwhelmed by the beauty!" Gabriela pressed one hand to her mouth.

A man with a rotund build, shaggy brown hair, and twinkling eyes, wearing a paint-smattered smock and holding paintbrush in one hand, turned around from the painting and grinned. "What is this, Gabriela? Do you speak in riddles again? Of course you have seen this before, but I am pleased that you approve of the progress."

"I do not know why I say the things I do at times." She dropped her hand and smiled. "Of course I have seen the painting before."

"Come help me with the goddess's apparel. I thought to make her chemise transparent, as you suggested, you naughty girl, but what do I know of ladies' clothing? That is why I consult with my neighbor, yes? Come and give me advice, my little seamstress to the goddesses."

Gabriela stepped forward and, as she did so, Brooke forced herself into the background to listen and watch. "I do love your Venus, Sandro, and am delighted that you have garbed her in my suggested gown." Her sketch still hung tacked to the easel's wooden frame. And it never ceased to amaze her how the master could create the illusion of transparent silk pearly against that luminous skin, skin so soft and glowing it was as if the breath of the goddess truly moved within, how he could take her drawing and fashion them on the body of a goddess.

The gown had been rendered with perfection, right down to the scattering of embroidered blossoms strewn across the over-gown, also created to look like transparent silk—many layers, each lovely, each shielding the languorous body of Venus while revealing her shape in a tantalizing manner.

Gabriela would have blushed once at such displays of near nudity but not now, not after she had spent so many years under the Medici roof discussing art and poetry, mingling with the master's other protégés. Now, she saw the human form as beautiful and worth celebrating rather than shameful and something to hide.

"It is perfect but for one small detail. Here," she said, pointing to the neck-line, "in truth, the stitches would gather the fabric to almost imperceptible ripples like wind upon water over which the silk flowers appear in merest floating buds of pink. As gorgeous as it is, it lies too flat." She faced the painter with a bold gaze. "I could bring you another chemise to use for study."

Sandro gazed the canvas before nodding. "No need. I have caught the image in my mind's eye as surely as if it hangs before me and will replicate it as per your suggestions. Yes, I can picture it just so and will make the changes immediately." Turning away, he placed his brush in a cup and gave Gabriela a quick hug. "Ah, my little creator of goddesses' apparel, thank you once again."

"You are welcome!" she laughed, stepping away, her gaze sweeping over the six men at work on various paintings throughout Sandro's spacious studio. The shutters had been thrown open to the sun and, in the courtyard beyond, she could see other artists at work at their easels. But a quick glance proved that the one she sought was not among them. Her heart plummeted.

Sandro cast her a sideways grin. "So have you come to see me, truly, or a certain apprentice of mine? For if young Lippi is your intended host, I fear I have sent him off to purchase more lapis lazuli this fine morning. Had I known you would visit, I would have sent another. In truth, he was eager to go and I expect he will drop into the House of Domenico hoping to see a certain seamstress on his return trip."

"Sandro, do not tease, and I hope he has not visited my house this day for Father is off to see a client and Jacopo will not welcome him." It was as challenging to keep the disappointment from her tone as it was to keep her two suitors from one another's throats.

"No, he will not. Must you marry that tedious boy? Surely your papa will not force you, even in the name of maintaining his prosperous business. Young Lippi is turning into a fine painter, quite a master in his own right even at such a tender age, perhaps as good as his father or better still. Signore Lippi senior would box my ears to hear me say so but I believe it true. The boy will do well."

"Father thinks to preserve the success of our house by insisting that I marry Jacopo, yes, but he is also not pleased that Lippi junior was conceived out of wedlock, the child of a friar and a nun. He claims that is the reason he refuses to consider Filippino Lippi, that and his idea that painters are generally such a disreputable lot."

Sandro slapped a hand over his heart, laughter shaking him. "He wounds me! Disreputable, me? And this after the many hours your father and I have spent at the Medici table sharing stories over wine?"

Gabriela squeezed his arm. "Perhaps that is why he calls you disreputable. I have heard you reference your bawdy tales and love of drink often enough. Father does love your paintings and Lippi's, too, but he claims his apprentice is a more suitable match."

"How dull of your papa. I shall scold him when next we meet but perhaps our patron will help persuade him?"

"So I hope."

"Has your father agreed to let you sit for me as Lord Lorenzo requests?"

"Because the Magnifico requests it, of course, but only if is executed according to plan and only if the portrait follows acceptable rules and I wear the special sleeves."

"Well, of course it will follow the standard profile and naturally you will craft those sleeves. It is all about those sleeves! Have you a sketch of how you plan to create them?"

"I do," she whispered, tugging him away from one of his painters who appeared to be busy putting the finishing touches on one panel of a large triptych. But he listened intently, they all did. Every place had open ears these days and studios were among the worst.

"Father has installed a secret room behind one back wall," she said, lowering her voice until the artist had to lean in to hear. "Even Jacopo does not know it exists. It is the wall where Fili painted that mural and hid all traces behind a skirt of one painted citizen. You remember, the one you remarked on, loudly I might add, that Fili had been careless with his use of his green under paints?"

"That was only to keep the boy from becoming too full of himself. I thought he was showing off to you like a young peacock, adding flourishes while catching your eye. I may be an old fool but I was a young fool once, too. Besides, he insists on using green as an underpaint. Makes no difference what I say, in any case—he mostly laughs at me and does as he pleases."

"Nonsense!" Gabriela smiled. "He respects and admires you but wishes merely to find his own style, which he does."

"Yes, he does." He suddenly sobered. "He will leave me soon, Gabriela. Already he speaks of returning to Prato to work on a local church commission. He waits only to hear a word from you and, meanwhile, I attempt to anchor him here with this. Come, I will show you."

Sandro led Gabriela to the far end of the studio to where a large sketch sat pinned to the wall. She studied it for a moment, picking out the details of a man sitting at a desk, in his library perhaps, while his expression read surprise as if startled by a sudden revelation. The saint's deep red orange robe appeared to glow in the half-light.

"Saint Augustine at the moment he learns of the death of Saint Jerome?"

"You have been tutored well. That is it exactly. It is to be a companion piece to that renegade Ghirlandaio's Saint Jerome and worked upon opposite walls of the altars in our beloved Ognissanti. Ghirlandaio was asked to paint his fresco before they considered me, can you imagine? Though the Ognissanti is my neighborhood church, they request his work before they asked for mine."

"No doubt they thought you too busy with all your commissions, Sandro," she said while patting his arm.

"Hmph. Father Olio claimed it was because the holy fathers believe that my paintings put pagan goddesses before God. Really! There is no more devote man than me...at least, most of the time. In the daylight hours, in any case."

Gabriela suppressed a smile. "Or at least some of the time. I suspect they want you to restrict yourself to religious art like Ghirlandaio does and many of the other great artists of the city, but your new creations are so beautiful and sing with joy. Surely joy cannot be a sin against God?"

"That is the great question, is it not? How we have chewed away at that one over all these years and how we are no closer to forming a decision. That Ghirlandaio only paints devotional work and his art soon becomes tiresome as a result. Even his colors are as restrained as light shoved into shadow."

Eager to avoid another rant, Gabriela nudged him back to the topic. "And you say that this fresco in the Ognissanti will somehow bound my Filippino Lippi to Florence longer?"

"That is my intent. I insisted that I not be working on mine at the same time that Ghirlandaio paints his lest I catch some kind of sobering sickness and fail to be able to lift a brush as a result. I requested that young Lippi assist me. This is partially in honor of his father, who, in truth, taught me the fresco technique, but also because the lad is adept at frescos, no doubt thanks to his father also. The important point is that Fili has agreed to do so in his father's name and I shall hold him to it."

"You are a true strategist, Sandro!" Gabriela laughed. "Thank you!" Turning away, she caught sight of a finished portrait hanging in the shadows. "Who is that? It looks much like the Lady Simonetta Vespucci in ways but in others not so much, and I cannot help but notice that you have garbed the lady in one of my sleeves, too."

"That young beauty is of no one in particular but an image of female beauty itself. Yes, there is some of the late Lady Simonetta—a paragon of beauty if ever there was one—about the mouth and lips, but should you look closely, the eyes are yours alone."

"You flatter me."

"It is not the role of the artist to flatter but to enhance the truth, have we not always said?"

"We have always agreed in this. In the same manner that I clothe a woman to look more beautiful, more truly herself, so you work your magic with the brush to illuminate life itself. Still I am pleased. I am no beauty but gazing at your paintings makes me feel more so." She smiled up at him.

"Gabriela?"

"Fili!" She dropped Sandro's arm and half ran down the studio to meet the young man who had just stepped in through the courtyard doors with a bag slung over one shoulder. Just a few feet away, she stopped, reading his expression. "What happened?"

He stood dusty, hose torn and what appeared to be a blackened eye. "That creature your father keeps as a foreman dared refer to me as a mongrel when I dropped by to see if you were there. When he insulted my mother, I lost my temper and flung my bag at him."

"The bag of lapis lazuli? Filippino Lippi, that pigment is worth ten of that pile of bones Domenico keeps as an apprentice!" cried Sandro, striding forward.

"No worry, master. It is to be ground in the pestle, anyway, and I have just given it a bit of a head start. I flung my bag at him and then made a dash for it but he caught up with me just outside the shop."

"Why not bloody his nose, Fili?" called their young helper, Piero, from the upper balcony. "That's what I would do. Anyone says any insults to me and pow!" Piero was only twelve and tasked with running errands, making frames for the canvases, and general tidying up. No one believed for a minute that he would ever tackle any man twice his size.

"Because these hands are gold, as Master Sandro says," Filippino said, holding up the long-fingered hands in question. "I will not risk damaging them for the likes of Jacopo Sistino."

Gabriela's heart caught at the sight of him standing there slightly battered but unbowed, handsome in the way of her countrymen with a strong jaw, full mouth, and fine dark eyes. She longed to run her fingers through his curly hair but she knew that could not happen openly as long as she was promised to another, though they behaved differently when alone. Just one stolen kiss so far but it was enough to hold her.

"Perhaps I should bathe your eye?" she asked softly.

In response, everyone within hearing distance hooted and whistled. Not a good idea, then. Gabriela dropped her gaze. "Maybe not. I must return to the shop. Good day to you both." And with that, she turned and slipped from studio, her heart galloping in her chest.

7

A long room filled with early afternoon light pouring in from a row of tall windows, their shutters thrown open to the warm air. Beside each window a table overflowing with fabrics where workers sat heads down, stitching, embroidering, trimming. A line of mannequins along the inside wall, many wearing pieces of rich and colorful clothing that seemed to catch the sun in bands of color.

At last, the atelier! Brooke thought Gabriela would never transport her there at first, though having just witnessed Sandro Botticelli's studio should be enough for anyone. Still, knowing that she would finally experience first-hand the height of Renaissance craftsmanship in the making was such a thrill.

Only Gabriela was not moving. Something worried her, keeping her pulse high and her anxiety roiling. Brooke realized that time had passed since the visit to Botticelli's—weeks, months, years?—and something had happened.

What is wrong? Sometimes her thought communications worked, some-times not. At that moment, Gabriela only gave a sharp jerk of her head as if attempting to dislodge an intruder while memories flashed of hidden panels, Lippi's loving gaze, Lorenzo de' Medici's face, a secret so important that Gabriela dared not think about...a hodgepodge of disconnected images.

A man who appeared to be supervising the workers caught her eye and straightened. "Gabriela, there you are at last. Finally. Come, Luella struggles with her sparrows and you must assist."

Jacopo, their foreman and head apprentice, also the man her father considered Gabriela's intended, turned out to be a lean man of slight build with a pinched bony face and thin, shoulder-length light brown hair.

Gabriela stifled her impatience. He fixed her with that look she knew so well—half admiration, half desire, only one of which she'd ever accept—in a face that always struck her as unbearably ordinary, uncurious. Dull.

Hanging her cloak on the hook, she approached Luella, who appeared to be struggling over a flight of birds flitting along the hem of a blush-colored velvet gamurra.

"They must be couched beneath in order to pad the little bodies, Luella. I have showed you the way in this. Why do you falter?" Gabriela lifted the fabric to study each little body, each tiny wing. The first ten were done to perfection under her watchful tutelage while the last five looked like broken creatures about to tumble to the earth. One appeared to wear a beaky frown.

"I tried, Gabriela, truly I did, but as soon as you are gone, I struggle," the girl explained while nearby the senior embroiderer, Signora Vespa, listened in with pursed lips.

"Which means that your mistress should remain by your side rather than disappearing for hours at a time visiting painters, or traipsing around the Medici piazza as if she were a noble lady instead of a tailor's daughter," Jacopo said with a frown that seemed to purse his face like a prune.

Gabriela shot him a sharp glance before laying a hand on Luella's shoulder. "You are a clever embroiderer who will not gain confidence as long as I hover over you. Now pick out those stitches and be careful to pad the bodies as you've been shown. The lines to follow have been clearly drawn but make certain to work over the holes so they do not show. Luckily velvet is a forgiving fabric. I will check on you within the hour."

Turning next to Signora Vespa, whose eyes darted back to her work, she added, "And, signora, I would appreciate you assisting Luella if you see her in difficulty."

The woman did not look up. "I have been told by the young master to mind my own work and not that of lesser embroiderers."

"Truly?" said Gabriela, rankling. "Then perhaps you'd best not listen in with so much interest to conversations that do not concern you, either."

She swung on her heels and strode toward the inner fitting area, knowing that Jacopo was sure to follow. Luckily the room was empty so Gabriela shut the door behind them. Ahead on the back wall, a gathering of painted citizens stood decked out in Domenico finery, all worked in Fili's expert hand.

"Why must you undermine me before the workers? Is it just to prove that you are master or are you attempting to shame me in some way?"

Jacopo's unshaven face flushed crimson. "I speak so to remind you that you are no lady, despite your airs. You should not be away for so long with no one knowing where you have gone. When your father is away, I am in charge."

"Says who? Never once has Father implied that you are any more than chief apprentice whereas I am head designer on par with and therefore not accountable to you."

"You are but a woman, clever or no, and your father gives you far too much leeway to do as you wish instead of what you are told. Even now that you no longer live with the Medici part of the time, you behave as if you do. Your learning corrupts you, as the priests claim."

"As the priests claim? Are you listening to gossip again or speaking of me when I have not granted permission? Do not attempt to rein me in, Jacopo Sistino."

"Listen to you! You speak as if you are lady of a villa—the airs! At times you act as though one possessed. I swear, Gabriela, the friars notice and speak of it among themselves. I have heard them whisper and I agree with them. I think you possessed, too. The things that come out of your mouth, and I do not mean the foreign tongues your father has allowed you to study under the Medici."

"What things?" she demanded but she knew before he spoke.

"They say that you have gained much corrupt learning from the dangerous notions of the Medici and their circle. That your father taught you to read, and that you have been further tutored with the Medici brood is in itself a sin for a woman of your station. You do not just read the Bible, but pagan books and poetry fit for drunken men. If this continues, they will demand that you be sent to a convent to redeem your soul. Listen to me, Gabriela."

Oh, dear Lord. She knew these things were being said yet she could not stop her behavior. It's true that she often felt as though she was possessed. "Rumors, you listen to rumors."

He reached for her hand, which she snatched away. "But, Gabriela, I will be your master once we are wed, which must be soon for it is not acceptable for you to continue this way and you are fully of age. I strive to protect you. I will not have you attend clients unaccompanied. Where did you go today—back to the Palazzo Medici or to see that renegade painter?"

"It is not your business, and what of your behavior when you struck a man who only dropped into this house to see me but a few months past?"

"He had no right to see you or you him. He is a mere painter and not worthy to speak to you when your father is not here. I am relieved that he has scuttled back to Prato where the whelp belongs! The son of a priest and a nun —it is shameful!"

"He was born in wedlock."

"But not conceived in wedlock. It is disgusting!"

"Oh, just stop!"

But he would not stop. He never stopped when in a headlong rant. "Now that Medici's wife and mother are dead and the daughters wed, there is no longer reason for you to attend him at his palazzo, either, especially without me. It is shameful that you do so. People are talking, and that Botticelli! It is said that he paints nude women and keeps a boy for his pleasure!"

She swung away. "You know nothing of the world, Jacopo. You judge by your ignorance, but I refuse to live so. It is not your concern where I go and whom I see and I will never be in your domain, regardless. You understand? I have not agreed to be your bride."

"But we were promised to one another as children and now that you are of age, you cannot just refuse me even if you have the patronage of the great Maestro Medici, who rules this republic as if a prince rather than a banker."

"Do not speak that way of Lorenzo de' Medici! He has brought this house more custom than we would ever have gained on our own."

"Yes, yes, the great Magnifico. He has turned your head and made you think you are of noble blood when you are not. For all your learning, you are no better than anyone else, Gabriela di Dominico. You are bound to me and that is that. I have yet to hear your father say otherwise, and until he does, I am your betrothed and in charge of your safekeeping while your father is away."

"To be a woman does not mean that I must be either servant or slave. Back off!" She stood stunned. Back off? Where did that come from? "I mean to say—oh, never mind. You do not own me." With that she turned and swept back into the workroom, which now hummed with companionable chatter.

"Jacopo, I have completed Master Folio's cloak," said one of the senior tailors, holding the red wool garment up to himself. "He has requested it immediately, yes? Shall I deliver it?"

Of course he shouldn't deliver it. They had a boy for that and young Tomo should be back shortly. She and her father made certain deliveries themselves only when the client was of a noble house and had requested such.

"You must stay and continue your work, Petro," said Gabriela. "You have still Master Folio's winter cloak to complete, yes? I see that it has been returned from the furriers." Gabriela looked pointedly at the sleek pelt that had been cut according to their specifications and now awaited sewing into the garment.

"Yes, do take it now, Petro," Jacopo interrupted. "Folio awaits it and I have promised it to him the moment it is complete, so go."

Gabriela turned away. Of course, that was a direct slam on her authority. To be undermined like that was damaging to both her and the camaraderie they had worked to create in their shop. The moment Father returned, she would address it with him. As much as he may desire the union between her and Jacopo, he would never tolerate that sort of behavior. Or so she hoped. In truth, he had changed much since her mother's death all those years ago—become more taciturn, withdrawn. At times, she felt she no longer knew him.

She strode down the long workroom floor toward the door to her house. Anger stirred so deeply she feared she might make matters worse by speaking more sharp words. She never knew what she might say or do anymore. Sometimes it felt as though she caged another within her chest and a lax moment might unleash the stranger.

Needing time to compose herself, she darted to the side door that led into the lower hall. She'd sent Maria to market so hopefully she'd have a moment's peace. There'd been little enough solitude now that Father had invited Jacopo to live with them. Every time she'd entered the library to study or read, Jacopo followed attempting to make conversation, though he had little interesting to say. She always tried to engage him in the kind of discussions she had been party to at the Medici palazzos and villas but it was to no avail and only angered him further.

Standing in the hall, she waited for her heart to still. There was so much to be done, all of it in secret, and she only hoped she was up to the task. To sin, to disobey, that was her path. Jacopo was only the latest complication. Tonight, she must find her way back to the Medici palazzo despite the risks, the scrutiny, the danger. She could only hope that Sandro would help, as promised.

What secret?

Voice pulled her from her thoughts. She called it Voice for lack of a better name but it had grown more strident of late, more demanding. This time it sounded so near at hand it could have come from beside her or nearer still, but that was mad—the hall was empty. She prayed it was not happening again, that sense that she was being followed by an invisible being who listened into her very thoughts, who interrupted her thinking with strange remarks that sometimes escaped her lips and seemed to know the future—Voice.

My name is Brooke.

My God, perhaps she truly was possessed? Sunday she would would pray even more fervently for her soul.

But I am sharing your soul. I am you in a future time. You are Gabriela and I am Brooke. We are together across time.

Gabriela swung around to stare down the empty hall, still deep in shadow. "Who are you? Why do you haunt me?"

In my life, you haunt me. I see things that are not there, do things that make no sense, just like you do. What is happening to you in your life is happening to me in mine. Somehow, past and future have tangled our lives together. We share the same soul.

"That is impossible!" Gabriela cried, leaning back against the wall. "That is ungodly, unholy! You must be the devil!"

I am not the devil, Gabriela. I am part of you, and what do we really understand of God when it comes right down to it? Only what the priests say and they are only men. Why do we allow men to be our interpreters of all that is good and evil? They hardly live blameless lives.

Gabriela thought back to some of the cardinals whose behavior had always been questionable, the friars, too. Look at that bishop who was a chief plotter in the Pazzi conspiracy and hung from a window for his trouble. His actions killed a man. Was he worthy to judge her?

Exactly.

"You can read my thoughts and see inside my head?" Gabriela whispered.

And you can do the same with me if you try. You are doing it now. You've been glimpsing my world in flashes. The men with the strange breeches in the Piazza della Signoria? That was in my time five hundred years into the future.

"Five hundred years in the future!" Gabriela pressed her hands against her lips, overcome by the enormity of it all. "I must be going mad!"

Neither of us are mad. I thought so, too, was under care of a doctor for a time, until I realized the truth, but now I believe we will both go mad unless we work together somehow. We must help one another, Gabriela. If we don't, neither of us will be free to live our lives and may even descend into true madness. Let me help you.

"Help me how?"

I'm not sure yet. For now, let me talk to you and you to me. Explain what is happening in your life—so much of it is foreign to me and only words in history books —and let me share mine with you. Maybe that's how we get through this. Maybe there's a time rift we need to heal to move on.

"A time rift?" Gabriela tried to laugh. "I don't even know what that is. It's another one of those words you pop into my head that have no meaning."

We travel new ground here, Gabriela. Let's do it together like the soul shadows we are.

Soul shadows? It was mad and yet nothing that had been happening to her of late made any more sense. Except this. Gabriela ran a hand across her forehead. She had been taught to regard the world with fresh eyes and must do so again. "Yes, yes. Let us go forward together."

"Who are you speaking to, mistress?"

Gabriela swung around to find Maria standing ladened with baskets staring at her, mouth open. How much had she heard?

"To myself, of course," she laughed.

The woman stepped forward, fixing Gabriela with a wary eye. "Are you certain the madness does not take hold again? The master says I am to watch for times when you speak to someone who is not there. It is a sin to speak to Satan."

"But I am but talking to myself, I said, and I am standing right here." Gabriela smiled, trying to appease the woman. Was everyone who surrounded her a spy?

"But the church says that talking to yourself is the work of the devil. Master Jacopo fears you are possessed."

Were they all discussing her now? "Do not speak such foolishness. Now get about your work and I shall return to mine."

As Gabriela strode down the hall toward the workroom, her soul shadow —soul shadow!—spoke in her head: *Maybe everyone here is a spy conspiring against you. Maybe you need to placate Jacopo somehow in order to calm him down and make him less of an enemy. What good is it doing you to egg him on? He could be dangerous.*

"How do I placate him?" she said aloud.

Oh, come on. You can figure that out: make it seem that you have seen the light and are chastened by your behavior and will attempt to be a better woman. I know it's goading but if you continue to buck his manly pride, he may do something horrid. Where do women go who behave in ways frowned on by church and republic, anyway?

"To the convent where they'll pray from morning till dusk, at best." Public humiliation, at worst.

"To the convent, mistress?"

Gabriela glanced down at Signore Malachite working on a cloak at the table to her right.

"Yes, I just remembered that we have an order to prepare," she said quickly. That wasn't true, of course, since most convents did their own stitching but for important vestments and altar cloths. Hopefully he did not know that. Since Ricardo Malachite was among the few who fixed on his own work, he would soon forget the discussion. Regardless, she had to stop speaking aloud.

Yes, you must, Brooke told her.

I am not accustomed to having my thoughts address another.

I am not another. I am you—your inner voice.

Gabriela sighed and strode down the aisle between the tables, stopping briefly to check on Luella's birds. "Much better," she said, leaning over the girl's work.

It still looks a little wonky to me.

Wonky? What is wonky? Never mind. I can guess the meaning and, yes, it still looks wonky. "Luella, though you have much improved, you must try again, this time take more care with the wings," Gabriela said.

"Yes, mistress."

"Wonky" is an English word that is part of my language in Canada.

Where is Canada?

Across the ocean.

A sail of many weeks?

I didn't sail, I flew on a mechanism somewhat like a big bird that your Leonardo Da Vinci might dream up.

Gabriela paused midway down the aisle, transfixed with thoughts of flying machines and Signore Da Vinci. *What kind of future is this?*

An amazing one but yours is no less spectacular.

"Gabriela, are you well?"

She turned to see Jacopo studying her. Flashing him a brilliant smile, she took his hand, tugging him back into the side room where she shut the door again.

Let the placating begin.

"Jacopo, forgive me for my temper earlier. Of course you are right to question me for I know my behavior has not been right as I dash out for this and that assignment yet tell you nothing. It is because I have promised to keep a secret while also I worry about Father's absence. It has been many weeks since last he wrote and I grow concerned."

Concerned with good reason, for he was about Medici business, too, which was dangerous enough.

Medici business?

Hush! Do not distract me.

"Why did you not speak sooner?" He took her hands. "Of course you worry but his visit to Venice keeps him very busy. Did he not warn us such?"

"Yes, but Father has always kept up his correspondence and when he fails to do so, I panic. First, I lose Mama and I cannot lose Father, too," she said, stifling a sob. Perhaps she played that a little too strongly but Jacopo responded best to her in distress.

Good thinking.

But it is so false.

Better to be false and function than to tell the truth and live in a cage.

"But, dearest, it will happen someday, as well you know, and when it does, I will be at your side to guide you through life as a husband is wont to do. Now, tell me, what was the nature of the note that arrived from the Medici palazzo yesterday? It is unseemly."

She was to visit the palazzo that night. Gabriela dropped her eyes. Best to lie than live in a cage. "The Magnifico wishes to create a special gift for his eldest daughter on the occasion of the birth of her first child," she said, "a set of sleeves to rival all others. It is to be a surprise and he requests I come in person to assist with the design. He is in pain and does not want to leave the palazzo yet wishes to be involved in its creation." That was all true, at least in part. She lifted her gaze to meet his eyes, half pleading for understanding, half driven by determination. "Our house cannot refuse him. He is still our biggest patron and deserves our assistance."

"But why not send me? That would be more proper."

"I am the artist who he champions in ways that others would see as unsuitable. He celebrates my art despite that I am a woman."

He stepped back. "Which only strengthens your pride. Do you not see, Gabriela? This must stop. Women were made to create new life and raise children, not to draw fine pictures for ladies' apparel. Your father humors you and Magnifico continues to strengthen the foolishness. Truly, you have talent but the Republic is tightening the restrictions on luxury wear as well as all other transgressions against God. If Medici wants something made, then I am who he must speak to. I will not permit you to go."

"And you think I am a transgression against God?" The words nearly curdled in her throat.

Careful, Gabriela. Pretend that you want to change.

But I don't want to change, I want to survive!

Then this is not the way and you know it. Pretend compliance.

What is compliance?

Obedience.

Meanwhile, Jacopo continued his tirade. "Yes—a woman acting above her station is an insult to God. A woman educated in pagan languages like Greek is an insult to God. God says so."

"The *priests* say so," Gabriela replied, attempting to rein in her emotions and listen to Voice—Brooke—but failing. To do so went against all her learning. She could not help but say what she believed to be true. "Are they not also reading ancient Greek and Latin? Do they not have fine libraries filled with such texts?"

Gabriela, be careful. This little man holds power over you. Work around him, not against him.

Jacopo waved his hand in an expression of exasperation. "Gabriela, listen to yourself! You speak heresy!"

"I speak the truth! How many priests and friars do we know who have sinned—prostitutes escaping their beds at night, mistresses of bishops so well known they are addressed in the streets! They dare speak of obeying God to us?"

Stop!

Another wave of the hand by the man who believed himself her master. "It is not for us to judge, but God! Pay attention to your ways or you will be punished, for you are neither bishop nor man but a mere woman. Soon the House of Domenico must obey the laws as must all citizens of the republic and the great Lorenzo will have no power to protect us then. His power wanes as we speak. We must make plain clothes, as is only proper—no more sinful shows of wealth and excess. That must become my role now when I assume management of the house. Once you become my wife, this will end and, in truth, it is best if you step down soon and return to household duties."

Gabriela turned away. Her greatest fear was unfolding before her eyes as she feared it would. Had she not seen the signs? Years of freedom under Lorenzo and her father—study, encouragement for her art and vision—soon to be squeezed out of her until she returned to the dull ball of servitude the church required. She could not bear that—life in a cage, existence without light and learning, without art!

Careful, Gabriela!

Gabriela clasped her hands over her ears as if that would stop the incessant voice. But she who lived within her was right: she must play the game. It was, after all, only one of many.

Lowering her eyes, she breathed deeply, relieved to find that it did clear her head. Turning around, she whispered: "I am sure you are right, Jacopo. Please help me to become a better woman, one who would please God and stop this gossip before the church takes action against me."

Gabriela's sudden change of heart worked. Jacopo's relief appeared to wash over him like a wave of sunshine. He was not the most intelligent of men. "Dear Gabriela, I will help you, of course I will."

"What shall I do?" Run? Hide? Soon enough, she feared.

"We will wed as soon as your father returns, perhaps even sooner. And you must pray in the meantime, of course, forgo those pagan texts and read the Bible only; be seen to worship our Lord as is only right and proper; stop going about unattended and never again to the Medicis' or the painter's house!"

A prison by any other name. Gabriela turned away to wrestle her panic to the ground. She must return to the palazzo that very night and nothing could stop the path she was to follow for she was bound by promise and Father also. And then there was Fili, dear sweet Fili, but at least Jacopo believed him gone from her heart as well as from Florence. But she needed, as Voice—Brooke— said, to play the game while retaining her freedom. Much needed to be done before that evening.

Suddenly, she had an idea. Swinging back to Jacopo, she struggled to smile. "Of course you are right: I must get myself in line and quickly, as you say. For that I need to reach out to God and hear the words of one I know not to be corrupted by the very world in which we live—the friar Savonarola. He speaks every day at a different piazza. I will attend and hear his words."

"*Perfecto!* The friar gathers followers by the thousands and preaches in different locations throughout Florence. Today he will be at the Duomo, I hear. His words are the way of truth and obedience to God. I will attend with you."

"You cannot," she said quickly. "Someone needs to remain here in the shop. If I am to cease being mistress in the workroom, then it is even more important for you to be seen as master."

"There is truth in that but you cannot go alone. You must go with Maria."

Maria, her house spy, and yet an easy enough keeper to slip away from in a crowd and slip she must. She had to ensure her plan was set for the night.

"Yes, Maria." Gabriela sighed. "I must attend his sermon this very day and take Maria." And hope to escape her keeper at the first chance.

8

The city bustled as always midday—the usual to-ing and fro-ing of carts, wagons, horse and foot traffic, the sound of wheels and hoofs clopping and rumbling over the cobbles and people calling out to one another.

Gabriela and Maria huddled in their plainest cloaks of dyed blue wool, stifling in the summer heat yet also offering some protection against the scrutiny of strangers and dust alike. It was frowned upon for a respectable adult woman to travel in public unless accompanied by either a maid or a male relative, not that she let that stop her most days, but she always ventured out well-covered. Traveling such always made Gabriela wonder why her sex must hide away in shame while men were permitted to walk with head held high and bare, regardless of their status, noble or thief alike.

Because historically women are seen as a sexual temptation to men, which it is apparently our responsibility to curb, as if we alone are responsible for male behavior.

Even still in your future time? Gabriela asked.

The laws of men change slowly, especially when they are masked behind religion, politics, and custom. Power will always protect itself and men have traditionally been the ones in power. Women's situations have changed a lot in my time—I hope to show you just how much—but it's been a long time coming and we still have far to go.

But look at those women there—the prostitutes. Gabriela was staring at five women with bleached yellow hair and low bodices displaying the rise of their breasts as they stood on a corner calling out to every passing man. *I envy them their freedom at times.*

Freedom can be an illusion since they are most likely slaves in other ways. They'd probably give anything for a warm bed they did not have to share and a roof over their heads.

Voice—Brooke—had become more active in Gabriela's head but now she saw her as more ally than fiend. In fact, she craved the company at times. It was a relief to finally talk freely to someone, if only inside her own head. It had become so much harder to see her supporters lately, though she must try again tonight.

"Look, mistress, here comes a noblewoman from the Tornabuoni family by the crest, I believe," said Maria, tugging at her cloak.

Gabriela looked up in time to see what appeared to be a long tent of green silk fabric moving as if as one creature across the street. Five women by the number of feet moving beneath the hems, probably a woman and her daughters with servants, on their way to a service, perhaps. Even noblewomen—especially noblewomen—were not to be seen in public unless attending mass or on feast days and always accompanied. Lucrezia de' Medici had come from the Tornabuoni family, at least as rich and noble as the Medici at the time. How she missed the old lady. Though fierce, she was learned and wrote poetry and celebrated Gabriela's accomplishments in ways Lady Clarice ceased to do as time went along. Even for them, it seemed, the restrictions were becoming more pronounced of late so this family must have a compelling reason to break with tradition.

She would prefer to go on horseback but Chiara was old now and she had not the chance to purchase another mare—too busy, too distracted—but she would need one soon.

Could you raise your head so I could see better? Brooke asked.

No, it is not safe. I can lift my head once we reach our destination but not before. It is dangerous to meet a man's eye when one is a woman on the street.

It's still like that in my time.

I would have hoped that things would change.

Don't get me wrong, they have, at least where I live or at least in some ways, but a woman meeting a stranger's eye can still be miscommunicated. Other places are still repressed by beliefs thousands of years old which treat women as cattle or worse.

Gabriela shook the thought from her head, focusing instead on not tripping over loose stones or stepping into a pad of steaming dung. The air reeked in this part of the city. Cleaners came by to sweep the droppings for those areas where the wealthy trod—paid for by the rich wool guilds about the city —as well as on the squares and around churches but not here in the Ognissanti or on the Via Marinoni, which followed the Arno the whole long way, bridge by bridge. Once one reached city center, caught the glowing dome of the Duomo on the horizon, the going grew easier but no less fragrant.

Maria remained glued to her side as if expecting Gabriela to bolt at any minute but Gabriela suspected she was equally afraid to venture so far beyond their neighborhood. The borgo markets and public squares and fountains were the extent of her realm.

"This way," Gabriela urged. "And should you ever get lost in the town center, head for the river and follow it the full way until you reach the Borgo Ognissanti."

"But why would I get lost if I am with you?"

"Prepare for anything, just in case."

The church bells struck throughout the city eleven times and Gabriela knew they were approaching Santa Maria del Fiore by the streams of people joining them along the way. It was a shock to see how large a following the friar had attracted, his fervent sermons fast becoming the daily entertainment for rich and poor alike. Ahead, Gabriela glimpsed a sheet of moving green silk and realized that even the women of the Tornabuoni had gathered to hear the preacher, too.

Still, she was not prepared for the crowd. Maria clutched her hand and huddled near as they pushed through the bodies to find a safe place to stand. The Piazza del Duomo offered plenty of space to gather and yet it seemed as though the best spots were already claimed and every other measure in between. Fine litters where wealthy nobles perched filled the areas directly before the makeshift pulpit but every other available space crushed with waiting listeners. Gabriela had heard it said that the friar preferred to preach outdoors to accommodate a larger audience and to avoid the efforts of priests to control their congregations.

Tugging Maria by the hand, Gabriela navigated the crowd to duck beside a mounted man and thus stake a spot beside his horse. Here they could gaze between the restless legs of the fine animal ahead of them to a clear view of the pulpit. They heard an exhalation from the crowd as a brown-robed figure climbed up to the stand and demanded attention.

"Children of God, come hear my words, for I speak in the name of our holy Father. I stand before you to demand that you permit me to lead you away from sin. The reason why I entered religious life is this: first, I could not bear to see the great misery of the world, and second, it burdened me to see the wickedness of men, their greed. Look around you at those who are poor and struggle even while those with full bellies and more than they need stand beside them. I ask, is this right, is this just, is this godly? And the rapes, the adulteries, the thefts, the pride, the idolatry, the vile curses. Has the world come to such a state that one can no longer find anyone who does good?"

Gabriela caught her breath. The friar's expression in a face so unattractive yet so alive with fervor that it hardly mattered spoke the truth into every ear. The rich suck the means away from the poor. Or did they? Did not the poor benefit from the rich, too?

"I am the hailstorm that shall break the heads of those who do not take shelter," the preacher was saying, and there were some around them that appeared to cringe at his words,

What an orator that man is! I can see why he changed the course of Florentine history.

"He did?" Gabriela whispered, but no one nearby paid her any mind including Maria, who was so in thrall that she had dropped Gabriela's hand and stared at the preacher with her hands clasped before her heart.

He did briefly but nothing ever lasts. Why do you need to see Medici tonight?

Later. First, I must seek out Sandro for he must go, too. Let me concentrate.

Brooke fell silent as Gabriela awaited the moment of her escape. It came much more quickly and easily than she imagined, for it soon became clear that she could probably set a fire in the piazza and no one would notice since the preacher possessed the crowd that completely.

In moments, she had slipped away from Maria and pushed through the press of bodies aiming for the nearest street. She had just broken through the wall of people as Savonarola's words echoed in her ears as if addressing her alone:

"I counsel you to return to God, to live in the manner of a good Christian, to repent the past, and return to piety." She couldn't even accept that much if it meant returning to the darkness of ignorance, but his next words chilled her the bone. "Likewise, I announce to you that your life is near its end; that if you obey not my words, you will go to hell, and you will be brought before the judgment of God with no way to escape!"

Classic case of the evangelist as bully.

What is an evangelist bully? she asked Brooke, but Gabriela was so roiling with doubt and fear by then that she could not focus on the response. Hearing those words storm out of the lips of the preacher caused her to falter. Maybe she was consigning her soul to hell and had best return to the fold, but at what cost—betray the great Lorenzo, crush all the light that warmed her, consigning her to dust? She could not live without art. Did that make her a sinner?

No! Words are a powerful tool, especially when brought to life with such fervor as that guy does, but that doesn't make Savonarola right or any less a tyrant.

"A tyrant?" she whispered. "But he's storming against the tyrants."

He is just a tyrant of another sort made more dangerous because he truly believes his own words and speaks the truth in some ways while twisting them in others. In the end, he's demanding to get his way and his mistake is in slamming everything that brings people joy—art, poetry, beauty. How can joy be a sin?

"I agree! How do you know so much?" Gabriela had paused at the corner unseen by any passerby, each intent upon their own business.

Because Savonarola is history to me. I know where he made mistakes and what happens to him.

"What does happen to him?" Gabriela longed to know yet did not. It seemed wrong to eavesdrop into the future somehow, yet what did it matter if Voice truly was from another century? She felt Brooke hesitate and knew she was having qualms, too. "Leave it," Gabriel whispered. "For now I do not want to know."

And for now I won't tell you. Just know that Savonarola is judged harshly in my time but, like most of us, he was neither good nor bad. Just human.

"I can tell that you are holding something back. He comes to a bad end, does he not?"

Bad enough. You live in a cruel and brutal time.

"Do I?"

Yes, but in ways, mine is just as cruel only in a different manner. By the way, I flit in and out of your days not always knowing where I am in your lifeline. You mention Sandro Botticelli, but the last time I saw him through your eyes, you were visiting his studio at the same time that Filppino had been slugged by Jacopo.

Gabriela's footsteps faltered. "That was years ago. Fili has been gone from Florence for years but we remain secretly promised to one another. We must be together. He awaits me in a secret place where we will be wed, should I survive this."

Survive what? What are you involved in?

"I have trained myself not to speak of it or think of it lest I reveal in error something that must be protected at all costs. So much depends upon my success. Do you know how I die?"

No, and I'm glad I can say that truthfully. The only future I know is what has been written down in history books, which means that only the famous and most notable are mentioned. I couldn't find any mention of a Gabriela di Domenico in the archives I dug through but found mention of your father being a tailor at this time, that's all. Women, for the most part, are forgotten in history.

She felt Gabriela's relief wash through her. "That is as it should be—the part about my life. I do not wish to be in a history book. If I do my task well and it remains untold, it will be because I have succeeded. Come. I must drop in briefly to Sandro's studio and then return home before Jacopo's suspicions rise."

They continued on their way, Gabriela preoccupied with her tangled thoughts. Brooke felt as though she was along for the ride, gawking at sites she never believed she'd see with borrowed eyes or otherwise. And the smells! Horse dung and raw sewage one moment, spices and street-side vendors and bakers passing with mounds of fresh-baked bread the next. A woman crouched by a corner selling tarts, and several of the lanes they rushed down seemed geared to dispense tankards of ale or glasses of wine through long open windows. Men called at Gabriela but nothing broke her stride.

At last they reached what Brooke recognized as the Ognissanti neighborhood, dominated as it was by its magnificent church even though parts appeared almost slum-like.

Your borgo seems very poor, said Brooke.

"It is perhaps among the poorest but some wealthy nobles share our church like the Vespuccis around the corner. The area looks even worse now. Many of our neighbors died during the plague, and had not the great Medici sent my father and I to the country, perhaps we, too, would have succumbed."

Did you go and live with the Medici in the end?

What do you mean "the end." I have not reached my end, but yes, I have lived for many years in intervals with the Medici, learned from the tutor Father calls Poliziano along with the other Medici children, most of whom I do not like, by the way. They taunted me for being a mere seamstress and laughed that I am not able to wear the rich clothes I create all while I was growing up, but they were a little afraid of me, too. The eldest son, Piero, is very weak but kind also, but many of the daughters are vicious. Their mother, the Lady Clarice, tried to curb their behavior but, in truth, she did not approve of my learning, either. The great Lady Lucrezia was another matter. I always felt as though she saw me for who I was and championed me wherever possible.

So, you are how old now and the year is?

I am too old—nearing on twenty-three years and still unwed—and the year is March 1492. How can you not know this when you know everything?

I don't know everything. I am being carried along inside your life and sometimes appear in new chapters without knowing where I have been dropped.

Stop chattering now. I must find my way.

Gabriela kept to the shadows, avoiding any passing glance until she turned a corner and was standing across from a tall stark building like so many of those that populated Florence. Tossing her hood closer around her head she slipped across the road and darted down the tight dark alley between the buildings to enter a bright courtyard lit by sunshine filtering through the trees. Brooke didn't recognize Botticelli's studio at first.

"He hardly lives here anymore. Sandro shares a house in the country with his brother and does not always come to the studio," Gabriela said aloud as she tossed back her hood. "I sent word for him to meet me here and I pray that he comes."

Gabriela pulled a key from her pocket and shoved back the lock before pushing the door open to step into the darkened studio. "He allows me to keep a key and to use the studio whenever I want. Sometimes I hide things here, but once when I came with Father, we found men living here and Father chased them away. Now I always worry should they return. I hide messages to him here and he to me. Fili writes to me through Sandro, as well."

Minutes later, she had flung open all the shutters to reveal a tired, paint-stained room with not a single painting or easel remaining.

Where has all the art gone? Brooke exclaimed.

"He has hidden some paintings about the studio but I know not where. I promised him I would not search about for them because they are not the kind of paintings he likes to display now. He has changed. You will see."

This must be about the time when his work returned to being mostly devotional.

"It is true that he paints mostly religious subjects now. I love his Mother Marys the most."

Though Gabriela seemed content not to seek the paintings out, Brooke couldn't help but peer into every corner in each direction that Gabriela looked. "Stop that," she said. "I made a promise."

But I didn't. This is one of the most famous painters in the history of art and there aren't many people who don't know him by name. To think that there may be hidden paintings about...

"People in your time speak of Sandro?"

Botticelli.

"They know him by his nickname?"

THE SPIRIT IN THE FOLD

Yes, and many revere him as I do. You don't know what a thrill it is for me to actually meet him through you.

"He would be shocked to hear you say that, for he is not as much in favor as he once was. It depresses him to see how other artists like Signore Da Vinci and Signore Simoni receive all the praise."

"What is this about Da Vinci? Gabriela, you of all people dare speak his name under my roof?"

Gabriela swing around. A man was striding into the studio. "Sandro! My voice tells me that you will become very famous in the future and perhaps the maestro Da Vinci will not overshadow you then."

"Your voice?" he said, lighting a lantern suspended from a hook. "Is she back again? I thought she no longer plagued you."

"She comes and goes but now has returned more loudly than ever. She says she is from the future and that we must work together lest we both go mad. Her name is Brooke."

Sandro Botticelli, now a middle-aged man florid in the face and expanded in girth, came fully into view under the lamplight. The weariness in his eyes and the downturn to his mouth startled Brooke. "It is perhaps best that you do not speak of such anymore, Gabriela, for as Magnifico weakens, so does your protection in Florence. A new world is upon us."

"I know this, Sandro. I heard the preacher speak in the piazza today and his words terrified me. Still, I am prepared to do what is necessary. Tonight, we'll finish our work and it will be done, at least in part."

Sandro shuffled over to a far wall where once had hung a myriad of paintings so glorious they had nearly brought Brooke to tears. Tapping a panel, a little hatch sprung open and he removed a roll of parchment.

"Here is the sketch that must go with us tonight, but I have something else for you, in part a promise and in part a gift, when the time comes." Unrolling the paper, he held up a sketch of a young woman shown in profile with her hair caught in a headscarf and the most glorious and intricate sleeves picked out in ink on paper, some parts as yet unfinished. The woman wasn't beautiful and yet her expression seemed to glow with some inner light that made her seem so.

"The sketch, and you made her in my likeness!" Gabriela pressed her hands together and Brooke could feel her face flush with pleasure.

"Once the dress is complete, I will paint a portrait from this sketch and leave it for you and Lippi as a wedding gift for when you return to Florence. That is if your mission is successful and you are able to return."

"But I must return someday. This is my home."

The artist regarded her sadly. "Gabriela, are you certain you know what you undertake in this? The Medici will not be able to protect you, nor your father, if he lives still, once you are away, and who knows when and if you can meet up with Filippino? Have you heard from your father?"

"No, nothing, though Fili sent a message to me through a passing merchant not more than a month ago. He waits for me still. As for my father, I have heard nothing and it worries me. I hope that the Magnifico will tell us where he was been sent. Sandro, forgive me. I forget myself. The wedding present—thank you. You know I have longed to have a work by you. It has been my dream!"

"But I have given you many smaller pieces, Gabriela, my thanks for your artistry, over the years."

"But once Father left, Jacopo sold them saying they were unholy and a shame on our family to have them hanging on the walls. But they were not his to sell."

"The clod. What a useless piece of donkey dung. He treats you as if you are his already and no better...no better than a woman. Has he—"

"No." Gabriela stopped him before he could say the words. "Even he would not dare. He will not touch me in that way until we are wed, which he means to do very soon. Jacopo will not risk his soul for a lewd act beyond the wedding vow, though I see plenty of unclean thoughts in his eye, I swear. Father has been gone for months and Jacopo hints that he may not return. In fact, I'm sure he hopes he does not. He will use that as an excuse to marry me soon."

Sandro rolled the parchment back up. "I am certain that he does think lewd thoughts for I have seen him flirt with a certain Venetian prostitute in the streets at times. But I will hide this sketch here after tonight just in case. Once the portrait is complete, I will secure it in a secret location that even the donkey dung will be unable to locate and will trust that you two young lovers can decipher what clues I leave behind after you marry. I have yet to determine a suitable place."

"Not here?"

"It is not safe."

"Not in the Medici palazzo?"

"No longer safe, either, as strange as that may sound. Never mind, I will find a very good location."

"Thank you. Now I'd best return home before Jacopo sounds the alarm. Meet me back here at eleven bells tonight?"

"Yes, can you bring your mount?"

"I have no horse able to carry me now. Chiara would not manage the cobbles."

"I will secure one, then. Be careful, Gabriela, seamstress to Venus. It grows in danger out there despite Friar Savonarola's pleas for decency."

"I know this to be true. Until this eve, Sandro."

9

$\mathcal{B}$rooke struggled to sit, surprised to find herself again in her bed only now it was dark. How much time had passed since the last twenty-first-century moment she had recalled? At that time, it had been morning and she had been on her way out the door to have breakfast.

Running a hand down her legs, she realized she was still dressed in the same clothes. *Hell, what have I been doing in my timeline while my mind ran with Gabriela in hers?*

Are you there now?

Brooke stilled. "Gabriela?" she whispered.

Yes, it is me at home in my bed as you are in yours. Only I think I must be dreaming.

"Don't be too sure. With what's happening between us, who knows?"

Take me for a walk in your century. Please, while we have the opportunity. I can see through your eyes that you are in a darkened room.

Brooke leaned over and switched on the bed lamp, sending the room alive with stark color. "This is the room my friend Enrico decorated—all white walls and simple furniture."

Decorated?

"That's what we call it when you fix up your home."

But Gabriela was now focusing elsewhere. *How does that lamp work? I did not see you light a flame.*

"Electricity. It would take forever for me to explain. Just accept it as a feature Da Vinci would approve of."

And what is that on the wall?

Brooke gazed at a modern painting from one of Enrico's favorite artists, Georges Braque—a jumble of blocks composed into a colorful composition. "Art," she said. "It's called a kind called cubism. Your Botticelli would be shocked, I think. It still startles me, but otherwise, does this room look that much different from yours?"

Are you too poor in your age not to purchase richly carved tables and chairs, nor tapestries or accomplished art? Do people show paint upon a board in your age and call it art?

Brooke snorted. "Sorry, that snort wasn't very genteel of me but the owners of this house are actually very rich; however, their tastes are different. Only one of them prefers a style we consider very modern and minimalist, the other is more traditional. Minimalism is like the exact opposite of the rich, luxe world you live in, by the way. Here, look at what I'm wearing." Striding over to the wall mirror beside the bathroom, she flicked on the overhead light.

Gabriela seemed too stunned to speak. *But you don't even look like me! And your clothing—what do you wear?*

"Pants in velveteen, which is the poor cousin to your silk velvets, and a turtleneck sweater in cashmere. I'm fairly well-dressed for my time where women often wear trousers and save skirts mostly for special occasions. Like our furnishings, our clothing is simpler and more streamlined than yours and we have lots of freedom to change things up as we like. Women are not forced to cover their heads when in public and we have plenty of freedom to go where we want, or at least in many countries we do."

Oh...take me through your home, please.

"Not my home. I'm visiting friends. I used to be a seamstress, too, by the way, only women are also called designers in my age. We're considered as significant in our field as men and our numbers are growing. I want so badly to return to my art and my life but first we have to resolve what's happening between us."

You are a seamstress, too? Why have you never said?

"How do I say anything about my life when I am hurling headlong through yours? And the word 'designer' is key, because in your time there was no word for a woman who created clothes from concept to execution. Gabriela, we are both designers, you and me." Brooke opened the door into the hallway, relieved to find it quiet and still, with everybody still in bed. "Let me give you a tour," she whispered.

Of all the rooms they strolled through, Brooke was careful to avoid the wing that held all the bedrooms; the one area that caused her time tourist the most excitement was the kitchen. It was so totally foreign to Gabriela that her questions kept on coming.

What is this?

"Something that browns bread in minutes. We call it a toaster."

And this?

"A cappuccino maker. It makes foamy milky coffee."

What is foamy milky coffee? Never mind. And that?

"That is like an oven in a box that can cook whole meals in minutes, like a potato in ten minutes. A microwave."

That is impossible! You live in the age of miracles. Is there nothing in your cook house that I would recognize?

"Forget the kitchen for a moment. Let me show you something that has come forward from your time almost intact."

Brooke left the kitchen to enter the rooms that lined the long balcony in floor-to-ceiling glass. There lay Florence in all its uplit glory, as beautiful a city, surely, as it was five centuries before, the golden dome of the cathedral holding court over all ablaze with spotlights.

Gabriela's gasp was audible. "The Santa Maria del Fiore exists still?"

"It exists almost exactly as it was in your time, a little worn in places, of course, but you would recognize it inside and out as you probably would most of the city. Little has changed. More traffic, certainly, and Florence spreads wider with the most recent buildings on the perimeter. Oh, and all but one of the bridges have been replaced. You can see the Ponte Vecchio way over there, or will when the sun comes up."

"I am heartened and amazed! To know that it survives across all these centuries gives me hope!"

"Florence is the epitome of the Italian Renaissance, the center of art and design, and even to this day, we celebrate your artists and thinkers as among the greatest of the known world—Michelangelo, Leonardo Da Vinci, Sandro Botticelli, Filippino and his father, Filippo Lippi, and it goes on and on. We still marvel at what occurred in your time, what happened to create such an explosion of brilliant art, architecture, philosophy, and literature. Do I sound like a tour guide or do you even know what that is? Your age is the age of miracles, Gabriela!"

"But how, why? There is so much violence, so much poverty and suffering."

"And there always has been and maybe always will be because we can't escape the bad part of humanity which you probably think of as evil, but still your time is different. Historically, we think what makes your period so extraordinary is all your brilliant patrons like Lorenzo de' Medici and his grandfather, Cosimo, who allowed the light of ancient learning to mingle with what had previously been the grip of a religious conviction that excluded all else. Science, exploration, discovery—that is the beacon that led your age through what we call the Middle Ages into a new dawn."

"But does that mean that there is no Bible in this new dawn, no God in your day?"

"Of course there's God but the universal power goes by many names and may be worshipped in many ways. Now many accept that there is not such a difference between one belief and another if love and light are the guiding influence in all. Your age and many centuries to follow persecute one religion over another, some with atrocities that it still shakes us to remember them. It's still happening in our day regardless of the religious beliefs of the perpetrators. How can we slaughter, burn people at the stake, hang and torture in the name of Christ, Allah, Buddha, God, and yet we do over and over again? Religious men make the most brutal warriors. How can any thinking being say that makes sense?"

The sound of clapping caused Brooke to turn, finding Felix standing at the doorway.

"You sound so ardent, Brooke. I had no idea you felt so much passion about comparative religion and the Italian Renaissance." Flicking on a table side lamp, he stifled a yawn. "Am I to understand that you are talking to somebody not from this century?"

"Felix! Yes, I have Gabriela here with me. We're actually communicating. I've just been giving her a tour. Gabriela, this is my friend Felix, who lives in this century, too."

But now Gabriela seemed distracted again, even confused. "But where are the mounts? We cannot go through the streets this night on foot."

"No, please. Not again," Felix muttered.

Gabriela stared at her friend uncomprehendingly. "Where are our mounts?"

SANDRO STEPPED FORWARD. "I have secured a wagon. You will need to hide in the back buried under a sack of rags. That way you will not be seen."

Brooke stared at Felix. "What did you just say?" She did not want to—

absolutely, desperately, did not want to—slip back into the past just yet but knew she was helpless to stop it from happening.

"Come, there is no time to waste. Magnifico is expecting our arrival before the bell rings midnight."

And then the room fell away and they were rattling down the streets of Florence in a horse-drawn cart, the city dark now but for the occasional torchlight or brazier burning beside a villa. Gabriela peered out from under a foul-smelling blanket, ducking down at the sight of anyone else out that late.

More cutthroats roamed the streets now than ever before and it seemed that no number of the men charged with keeping the streets safe could stem the tide. The bands of thieves roamed all over the city. After years in power, Medici's republic was crumbling again.

Sometimes I think it happens to all governments, eventually, Brooke mused.

Gabriela did not reply, either because she was too fixed on her plans that night or couldn't dial into her time tourist's thoughts for some reason. Either way, it left Brooke feeling both unanchored and frightened. What was happening to her body back in her century? What if Gabriela should die or have some terrible accident while she was trapped inside her life? Gabriela seemed to be on a trajectory nobody could stop. But then, she thought with a jolt, that was what must be because it had already happened.

When something slammed into side of the wagon so hard that the wooden slats shook, even Brooke pulled her attention fully into the now. Oh, my God! They were under attack!

"Let go of me!" screamed Gabriela as two men jumped into the wagon and began tugging at her clothes. Being on her back put her at an immediate disadvantage.

Shove them off! Brooke told her. *Not like that, like this!*

She kneed one in the groin. Grunting, he pulled back, which gave enough time for the next one to land on top of her. For that he got a thumb jammed into one eye.

"Hey, lads, we have a fighter here!" cried another one, shoving the blinded one out of the way. How many were there—three, four?

"We love them frisky, don't we, lads?" said the one gripping his injured groin. "No need to be gentle with the likes of that."

"Goin' off to see yer client, are ya? Let us have a little taste first!"

"I am not a prostitute!" Gabriela gasped as she struggled to her feet.

"Yeah, so why are yer out so late, then, missy? Fine ladies don't dollying off in a cart after-hours, do they? Is this yer dad taking you off to turn a few coins?"

Botticelli had half turned in his seat, feebly whacking at the attackers with a stick while crying for help. Painters were no fighters so neither Gabriela nor Brooke held out much hope there. But Brooke knew a few moves of her own, as long as Gabriela passed over the controls, which, oddly enough, it seemed she had.

Lunging out with a fist to the throat of one bastard, she kicked out at another before whipping the stick from Botticelli's hand and bringing it down upon the head of the fourth thug to enter the fray.

By now they had attracted a crowd. Rather than helping the innocent, the bystanders were calling out bets on which party would win the fight—the single female and the useless man that attended her or the four drunken thugs after a bit of fun. It was clear who they favored.

Brooke was enraged. Every bit of self-defense training she had taken as a young woman came back in a flash. Even though Gabriela didn't have half the muscle mass of Brooke's own body after years of fitness, she still had the moves that worked on drunken idiots. A final kick where it hurts, the last lumbering fool tossed out of the wagon, and Brooke was yelling: "Move this thing, Botticelli!"

Sandro scampered back into the front and called for the nag to move, scattering the spectators as the wagon rattled off down the street.

"Is that the painter who paints all those naked sluts?" they heard someone cry out behind them, but Botticelli kept urging the nag into a lurching gallop until they were halfway across the Piazza della Signoria heading for the Medici palazzo.

"How did you learn to fight like that?" Sandro said over his shoulder as they slowed to a trot, the poor animal exhausted by now.

"I do not know," said Gabriela.

That was me. In my age, women can take self-defense classes to prevent rape and the like. It all came back to me.

"That was Brooke, my voice," Gabriela said, climbing up on the seat beside the artist. They were close enough to the Medicis' now not to fear attack, or so she hoped.

"Your voice can now order your corporal form?" the artist asked in surprise.

Gabriela shook her head. "Amazing, yes? Though I can kick and scratch like anyone, that was the first time. I found myself doing things I never knew I could do—or would even think about doing—like digging that thumb into that monster's eye. And, Sandro, earlier this evening—" she paused "—five hundred years into the future, I should say, I walked around an apartment like even you could not imagine, where silver boxes cook meals in minutes—"

"Stop!" Sandro crossed himself with his free hand. "This sounds like deviltry and I fear to hear it. Gabriela, you know this is not possible."

"How do we know what is possible until it happens?" That was Brooke speaking.

They carried on without further conversation until they arrived at the back gates of the Medici palazzo.

* * *

"WHO GOES THERE?" called the gatekeeper.

"Signore Alessandro Filipepi and Signorina Domenico. The lord expects us."

The gates swung open, the weary mare placed in the care of a groom as Gabriela and Sandro strode across the courtyard.

"When last did you see him?" Sandro whispered as he gazed around at the torchlit garden with its trimmed hedges and tinkling fountains.

"Not for many months," Gabriela replied. "When last we met, we worked out the designs for the sleeves. Magnifico had already obtained the fabric, which I smuggled into my secret room where I work upon it while the house sleeps. But for the sleeves, it is almost complete and, I swear, it will be my finest work."

"I am sure it is lovely, Gabriela, suitable for a goddess, and it is a shame that no goddess will wear it, nor see it."

"Perhaps that is not the way it will be." She said nothing more and the artist did not request further details.

"I so desperately crave a drink of the lord's fine wine."

"Perhaps it would be best to remain with water, Sandro. Tonight we need to remain clear of head."

For that, the artist only laughed while Brooke watched her surroundings in awe. To think that she entered the Medici palazzo in the company of Botticelli, who despite the glory of his art was all too human.

When they entered the main corridor moments later, Brooke studied every corner in Gabriela's peripheral vision. There had been such changes from her last remembered visit. Now Donatello's famous bronze statue of David dominated the marble hall but there were other sculptures and artworks about, too. She recognized pieces by Leonardo, Michelangelo, and Botticelli himself while other pieces seemed to be by known artists and yet she had never seen them before. "Wait! Is that painting of Christ on the cross a Giotto?"

"We cannot linger," Gabriela chastised as they followed behind the servant leading them down the hall toward an open door.

"I know this, Gabriela. I move as quickly as my old legs will carry me," Botticelli mumbled.

"It is not to you, but to Brooke I speak. She wishes to stop and look at this and that. She loves the art and sculpture so."

"Perhaps this voice of yours is not such a demon, after all, but still she makes me uneasy."

Let me speak to Lorenzo de' Medici himself, Brooke requested.

"Hush!" Gabriela cautioned.

They had arrived at a carved door on which the servant knocked. A raspy voice bid him enter, which he did, returning moments later to usher them inside before swiftly exiting and shutting the door behind him.

The room was stifling, with a fire burning in the grate despite the summer warmth. It was the library, Brooke realized, but it looked very different than the last time she saw it, much like its master. Though sconces and candles lit the room, the man who dominated the space seemed huddled into the shadows beside the hearth like some ancient hermit. Hunched down in his velvet robes, one leg propped on a cushioned stool, Medici was barely recognizable. A dour fringe of gray-streaked straight brown hair hung straight down over his brooding forehead, the dark eyes sparkling with intelligence above a mouth grimaced in pain. A book lay open on his lap, a goblet of wine perched on the table at his side, and a carved walking stick leaned within easy reach.

"Ah, Botticelli and Gabriela, you have come at last." He lifted a hand in greeting. "I feared that the streets might run with vermin this night as Florence festers with a plague of lawlessness."

"Yes, lord. We were set upon by scoundrels on our way here but somehow managed to shake them off." Sandro cast a quick glance at Gabriela, who appeared too overwhelmed to speak. "Savonarola preaches salvation if the rabble and good citizens alike will strive to return to God, my lord," Botticelli said, stepping forward. "So far, few listen."

"I have heard his thunder. Come inside and take a seat before me, both of you." Lorenzo de' Medici spread a hand toward the two chairs plump with silken pillows that had been pulled around the fireside. "Join me in wine. I have asked my man to pour you each a glass and the carafe is there for you to help yourself. As for Savonarola, I have heard him preach many times now and it seems that he holds me accountable for all the ills that have befallen Florence," Medici said with a wry smile. "Do you believe that to be true?"

"Of course not, my lord," Botticelli hastened to assure him while passing a goblet to Gabriela and taking one for himself. For a few seconds, he was too busy drinking to speak, which left Gabriela to fill the void.

"You are the undisputed master of Florence, my lord. What you and your family have given this city, no one can deny." Gabriela perched herself in the carved seat, took a small sip, and smiled. Though it was excellent wine, she would not drink too much, her goal being to complete her task as quickly as possible and return safely home before Jacopo knew that she was missing. Only six hours before dawn.

But then her mouth continued speaking. "We don't see you as the cause of Florence's downfall, sir. History proves that any city's rise and fall is due at least in part to the passage of time, changes in politics, wars, fading fortunes, and a whole complex suite of influences and circumstances. Florence will always be a great city of art and architecture and you considered a great man who helped one of the most important times in human artistic inspiration come into being."

Botticelli sputtered into his glass.

Gabriela slapped a hand to her mouth. *Do you mean to ruin me? Do not speak!* "I apologize, my lord. I do not know why I said that," Gabriela hastened to assure him, dropping her hand.

Lorenzo de' Medici studied her from under his fringe. "Nevertheless, your words are spoken with such authority that I can only hope that they bear some truth. You continue to amaze me, Gabriela. Are you still beset with visions and portents of the future?"

"Yes, my lord. My voice speaks in my head at times but please do not pay those words any mind. Sandro and I have brought the sketch tonight with hopes to complete our work so that we are prepared when the time comes. Have you heard from my father, my lord?"

"No, but in this case, not hearing word may equally assure us that he arrived at his attended destination with the treasure intact. He is disguised so not to attract notice."

Gabriela was not certain to what kind of treasure the Magnifico referred but since the Medici palaces contained so many riches, she could only imagine that a fortune lay in her father's charge. Hopefully being guised would offer some protection. "My lord, I ask that we quickly conduct our business so I can return home safely."

Medici nodded and sighed. "Just so. We must be quick about it. Where is the sketch?" He winced as he adjusted his position.

Botticelli took another swig of wine before reaching into his bag to pull out the canister. "Here, sir. There are only a few remaining sleeve details to complete the design."

"I have worked the gamurra and chemise, my lord, and the watered silk that you had requested for the sleeves is as perfect a shade of cream as you had hoped with the velvet of the giornea as soft and glowing as sun cupped within a rosebud."

"The color of light on a new dawn. Would that I could see what you describe to such perfection." Medici chuckled. "Your descriptions always lighten my heart. I think that you could be a poet, as I have said many times. The dress will look lovely on you, if by chance you get to wear it."

"My lord?" Botticelli asked, turning to Medici.

Lorenzo met his eyes. "It is my bargain with Gabriela that should she successfully fulfill this task and deliver the sleeves to the location as planned, the dress will be hers for the keeping, to wear at her wedding to Filippino Lippi, if that is still her desire."

Botticelli turned to his young friend. "Is this your heart's desire, Gabriela, not florins to assist you in your new life?"

"I will give her another payment, too," Medici remarked in his nasally voice, "but it seems as though it is the dress that holds the greatest worth to our young friend here and I do not mean because of any secret secured safely within the sleeves."

Gabriela flushed. "All my days I have sewn glorious dresses for other women the likes of which can never be worn by me or those of my status, no matter what my means. This is my art and yet I cannot lay claim to it. Once I escape Florence to meet up with Fili for my marriage, this dress will be mine on my wedding day. To don my own work for a single day will be thanks enough for any service I perform here."

"Young Lippi will not reveal our secret," Lorenzo said, "for Filippino has his part to play in this. It has all been arranged and those sleeves and the message they protect will remain safe if not one way than another."

Hearing his name brought a smile to Gabriela's lips. Her Fili, her heart's intended. Just thinking of him warmed her everywhere, made whatever risks she took or was about to take worth every treacherous moment. To marry the man she loved and work at her own art in freedom away from Florence had become her one burning goal.

"My young once-apprentice is in this, too?" Sandro asked.

Lorenzo nodded. "Yes, for the best secret is a tree with many branches. Should one branch be cut asunder, another will bear fruit. And now here, Gabriela, I will give you this to keep safe in case we do not see one another after tonight." Fishing a filigreed iron key from his pocket, he passed it to her. "The rest of your instructions will unfold in good time. This will be the final clue and I will trust you to grasp its meaning in time."

"I will hide it where we discussed, my lord, and should I be accosted and the dress damaged or stolen?" Turning her back, she dropped it down her bodice.

"Then I will have other layers of codes to tell my story, as I have said. Filippino has another piece and I trust him to execute it according to my instructions and his heart. You, my dear, will claim your dress in payment for your loyalty over the years and more besides."

Sandro stood before his patron with the sketch unrolled. "Here it is, my lord. All that needs be done is to complete the details."

"And then I will work them in my secret room away from prying eyes until the time of my departure arrives," Gabriela said. "The key will be hidden within the folds. I am eager to begin."

Magnifico studied the sketch and nodded. "Another marvelous execution, Botticelli, and you have captured our young friend here to perfection, right down to the gaze that is fixed forward as if on a horizon of possibilities. I have gathered emblems and researched symbols as I want included in our sleeve."

"And I shall embroider each accordingly," Gabriela assured him.

"Let us be at it, then. Sandro, use that table over there and I will describe the motifs as I envision them and show you my drawings of the symbols I desire." The lord struggled to his feet, grabbed his cane, took his wineglass in his free hand, and made his painful way to the table. "Certainly, the Medici crest must be present but I have given much thought to the other symbols that will help unlock my secret."

"There must be bees and flowers to wrap the code," Gabriela said, following the men over to the table. "Each flower to hold a meaning, each emblem a clue, and only together will they reveal the location. I recall exactly what we said, my lord, and have obtained the silks to work the motifs."

"Ah, good. The insects and flowers will make the untutored eye believe that they look upon adornment alone when the complete composition will hold a far deeper meaning." Lorenzo eased himself into a chair at the ornate oak table with a groan.

"Am I to know the meaning of the symbols?" Gabriela asked.

THE SPIRIT IN THE FOLD

"Some you will know, others not. Place the sketch here, Sandro, and we will watch you work."

The artist took another swig from his goblet, unwrapped a leather folio of pencils, and began to sketch each remaining motif, beginning with the Medici coin crest, which formed the center of the sleeve's embellishments. Each emblem suspended in the triangle frame of the lattice-like quilting that would run diagonally down each sleeve.

As Botticelli sketched, Medici and Gabriela watched, Brooke shoved way down into Gabriela's mind struggling to emerge. Unable to speak or assert herself in any way, it was a shock to discover just how easily her newfound freedom could be withdrawn by the force of Gabriela's will. But Gabriela was resolute, leaving Brooke no choice but to wait for the moment of distraction she needed.

The process appeared to take longer than Gabriela had expected because she shifted in her seat and flinched at every gong of the bell. "Is it possible to hurry, Sandro?"

"No, it is not," the artist grumbled, reaching for his goblet of wine. Magnifico and Sandro were almost at the bottom of their second decanter. "One cannot hurry precise execution."

"No, one cannot." Lorenzo nodded, his eyes partially closed. "The details are important. The details will serve as a trail for lovers of art and literature, for lovers all, and confound the enemies that conspire to destroy what we so deeply honor."

"When do you expect my journey to begin, my lord? I trust it will be soon," Gabriela asked. Whether the lateness of the hour, fatigue, or what, chill trickles of worry weakened her nerve.

"I know not," Lorenzo said, now studying the candlelight flickering on his goblet. "It may depend upon my health, whether I live or die and when. Certainly my enemies wish me dead but will they wait for the inevitable course of time to make their move? Will it take my actual demise for the walls to crumble and the throng to raze my home to pillage my possessions? Maybe tomorrow, maybe another course of the sun or several more—who knows?— but it will come, that much I am certain, and when it does, you must be away."

Sandro looked up. "But, my lord, you are a powerful man still, always. No one would dare."

Lorenzo waved a dismissive hand. "I once thought no one would dare to butcher my brother as if he were no better than a rabid beast instead of the fine man he was and yet it happened. Now I count on nothing and no one. That is why I have arranged this plan in segments, each one connecting with the next, none of it known to only one. Even the two of you, my friends, possess only a small part, though the illusion is that you know it all. You do not. This is for your protection."

"But how will I reach the destination, sir, if I do not know where I am to go?" Gabriela asked. She could understand not knowing the full nature of the plan but to set off on a journey and not know the destination?

"It will be revealed when necessary. Do not fear, Gabriela, my dear. I will have you well attended each step of the way." Lorenzo emitted a noisy yawn. "Botticelli, I ask that you accompany her for the first length as we have discussed, for which you will be paid handsomely. I have arranged for others to accompany her the rest of the journey."

"As promised, I will go with her as far as the hills of Fiesole and then create a ruse in case we are followed."

Lorenzo wiped a hand across his eyes. "Very good. If for some reason you cannot go, you must secure another and contrive whatever ruse best works. There is a Franciscan monastery where the abbot is still a friend. Hopefully he remains so when the time comes."

"How will I know when the time comes?" Gabriela asked, leaning forward, but her lips answered the question before she could tamp down the words: "Is it when learning and beauty burn in the streets of Florence?"

Lorenzo de' Medici turned toward her, clunked his goblet on the table, and lunged to his feet. "When learning and beauty burns? What portents do you hide from me?"

No, no, no!
"I do not know why I say these things!" Gabriela had slapped a hand over her mouth again as if that would stop anything.

"You do know why you say them! You say them because you harbor some voice that can foretell the future, which you hide from me. So you have told me many times before. Now I demand that you allow that voice to speak. When learning and beauty burn, you said. What is it that you mean?" Magnifico stood now, with hands bracing the table, his eyes glittering with either rage or pain, she could not tell.

"I know not, my lord. The voice spoke before I could stop it." She lowered her hand. Never had she seen him so furious—or drunk and so addled with pain.

"Do not muzzle it, Gabriela. Let it speak."

I cannot believe you have said these things. Gabriela sent her furious thought to Brooke.

He needs to know.

"Speak, I say!" Medici fumed.

Let me talk. I will be careful. The past is past and can't be changed no matter what I say.

"Does this burning occur when I am dead, is that it? Perhaps when once again the Medici are banished from this city and sent into exile, is that when the city will be sacked?"

Gabriela relented and allowed Brooke to take over.

"Not sacked, no," Brooke assured him, choosing her words with care. "Though you are right to fear your enemies, no one will burn this city to the ground, I promise you, at least not before my lifetime."

"Your lifetime?" Lorenzo de' Medici fixed her with deep-set eyes buried deep within his bony brow while easing himself back down to his chair. "Your lifetime….and what is your lifetime?"

Brooke forced Gabriela to take a deep breath. It was like the body they shared had forgotten how to breathe. "I come from the future."

Across the table, Botticelli dropped his pencil and crossed himself. "The devil, my lord, it is the devil!"

"I am not the devil," Brooke said crossly. "There is no devil except for what burrows into the hearts of men in the name of power and greed." Actually, she was pleased with herself for pulling up that line.

"A witch, then," the artist spat.

"No witch, either. Why is it that men can only define women as a witch, a Madonna, a goddess, or a whore? Every single woman that has ever lived can be all of those things and more besides but you label us with either one thing or another as if you can't work it out for yourself. Are you only one thing, Botticelli—only a good man or a noble one or a foul-talking beast sometimes, or are you human and a mix of all?"

"She argues well, this oracle," Lorenzo said, leaning forward, his face twisted in a grin.

"So does Satan," Sandro whispered.

Brooke stood up to give herself courage. "What do men in this age know of the devil except what the priests tell you? Are you so afraid to think for yourselves? I am a soul trapped in the life of another. I call myself Gabriela's inner voice because that's what it feels like to us both. In my own time, I exist as a real woman named Brooke. I travel off and on through time with Gabriela and she with me and only recently have we been able to communicate. Because of me, she's had knowledge of things to come but only because she reads my thoughts occasionally and now I speak them, too. For all I know, everyone who can divine future events hosts somebody from the future in their soul as we do."

"A miracle by any other name!" Lorenzo rasped, his expression more animated than ever. "From what year do you hail?"

"2022."

"You did not say 'In the year of our Lord,'" Botticelli muttered.

Lorenzo propped his elbows on the table to brace his head but the intensity of his gaze never wavered. "The year 2022?"

Botticelli had begun to pray under his breath.

Medici slammed one fist on the table. "Cease, Sandro! After all the years we have lived, can you still not recognize the truth when you hear it? We are speaking to the future. I swear, I will hear what the future has to tell me before this night is through!"

"Yes, my lord," Botticelli whispered miserably, reaching for more wine only to moan when he found the decanter empty.

"How do I die?" Medici asked. "Will I be slaughtered like my brother, burned at the stake as a traitor, perhaps dropped from my neck outside the windows of the Palazzo Vecchio like so much human rubbish?"

Brooke was ready for the question. "No, my lord. You will die from natural causes in your bed."

A tiny smile warmed his wide lips. "In my bed. That I consider a great blessing, one that does not often befall men like me. When?" he demanded.

"Is it wise to know the date of one's own death, sir?" Brooke asked him. "I'm not certain I'd want to know, if I had the choice."

"Does this mean that you do not know the date of your own death or even Gabriela's? How is that possible if you can see the future?" he asked.

Brooke could feel Gabriela tensing. "I can read the future only because I have either lived it or read what is recorded in history books. Over five hundred years have passed between your time and mine and a lot has been written on almost every major event, some of it contradictory. Plenty has been written about the great Lorenzo de' Medici, master of the Italian Renaissance, whose patronage of art, science, and literature is cited to be pivotal in the history of the world."

"Is that how I will be remembered?" Lorenzo's voice was filled with wonder, his eyes almost wet. They were buried so deeply under his misshapen brow she couldn't tell.

"It is, but I don't know the date of Gabriela's death because history doesn't consider her life important enough to mention, a common enough thing since men wrote the history books and most men don't see the actions of women worth recording."

Lorenzo burst into a bark-like laughter while Gabriela relaxed in relief within their shared body. Brooke knew how much her soul shadow dreaded knowing the details of her death and was grateful that she didn't know them to tell.

"That is the way of things between men and women," Medici acknowledged. "My mother used to rage against the unfairness of it all and took little comfort in the fact that God made the rules."

"Men made the rules because men transcribed the Bible. Power always wants to protect itself so power writes history to protect its interests." Brooke did not want to let this go.

"So you do not know how Gabriela dies. She is probably pleased that you do not but I, on the other hand, want the truth as to my own demise. Speak the date," Lorenzo commanded.

Why not tell him? He was ill and knew he could not continue forever. A man like him living in the age he did faced his death multiple times in multiple ways and never flinched. Brooke dropped back into her chair and clasped her hands on the table before her. "1492."

"I haven't long to live, then. No surprise. Where do I die?"

"In the Villa Medici at Careggi."

"My favorite abode. Where will I be buried?"

"In the Basilica di San Lorenzo here in Florence."

"No such place exists."

"There will be. A beautiful chapel will be designed by Michelangelo and built next to the Duomo where both you and your brother will be laid to rest."

Now there was no doubting his tears. The great man was sobbing noisily, while attempting to wipe his eyes on his sleeve. Reaching for his glass, he sobbed harder at the sight of the dregs and called out to his servant to refill the glasses. Within seconds the man burst in with a flask to refresh all the receptacles before quickly exiting.

Lorenzo and Botticelli both drank deeply for a few moments before the master slammed his glass down on the table and turned to Brooke. "And of what will I die?"

Another anticipated question. "They believe something called acromegaly, a rare disease which causes thickening of the skin and bones and promotes pain in your extremities as well as headache and fatigue."

"I suffer from all of that now if that is the description," he said. "Acromegaly...from the Greek 'akon' for extremities and 'megas' for great. Whatever its name, it is as if a beast inhabits my body and transforms me into something to which I was not born, but how in your time did they discover this to be my affliction?"

Do not tell him. It will be unbearable, Gabriela cautioned. Brooke didn't miss a beat. "They studied your portraits and could see the changes in your features and they guessed." Better to say that than to tell a Catholic man that scientists desecrated his grave.

"Ah, yes. Though I have never been a pretty man, still the artists paint my likeness." His gaze searched her face. "And what will become of Florence at my death?"

"In a word, Savonarola." At least, at first.

"Did you hear that, Botticelli? That preacher will hold sway in the end. Did I not always say?" He downed his glass and poured himself another.

"He will gain in power and authority and his sway will bring repercussions," Brooke said, "but you have prepared for them."

Enough! It grows late and I must be home.

"What repercussions, exactly?" Medici was slurring now, relaxed and clearly enjoying his conversation with the future, the sketch forgotten. Sweat beaded his bony brow. "Already the mangy little friar speaks of ridding Florence of what he claims are pernicious manuscripts written by the Roman and Greek pagans, which are more learned men than he. He strives to eliminate all art not of a religious nature, and in doing so, banishing all that I love. I was right to take the moves I have to protect my treasures. What we do here tonight is right and true." He took another gulp. "But, Gabriela, I move to protect you, too."

Gabriela couldn't fathom his meaning there. It seemed only that he put her at risk, but she realized that the man was ailing, that his treasure was more important than a mere human life. "Is this treasure what Father secures on his travels?"

Brooke gazed around her, recognizing for the first time that the shelves looked nearly bare. "The books! That's what you are protecting!"

Now they were sharing Gabriela's voice, which was bound to befuddle themselves if not their companions.

"Yes, the books, the manuscripts, the codexes, the scrolls. They have all been dispatched to keep them safe," came Medici's raspy voice.

"My lord, I beg you, let us complete the sketch so I can be away. Jacopo watches me now, and should he catch me out this night, who knows what he will do."

And from Brooke: "Savonarola will hold a huge bonfire one night in the year 1497 and urge the citizens of Florence to burn paintings, dresses, books —books! If you hadn't made to protect the treasures of the ancient world, little would have survived. This one act of yours may be all that preserves certain works of Socrates, Plato, and the other ancient philosophers and poets."

"But I will already be gone," Lorenzo remarked miserably as if suddenly realizing that the date of his death was not merely a concept but a pending reality. "I will be nothing but dust, memories in the heart, words on the page, nothing more." With that, he lowered his head upon the table and sobbed.

"You will be, but your legacy will live on," Brooke assured him, but she could tell that the great Magnifico was no longer listening. Drunk and lost in his misery. Seconds later, his snores reverberated the air.

"Let us finish the sketch, my lord. Only one remains, the wasp," Gabriela pleaded.

Forget that. He's gone for the night, Brooke told her.

And as if to prove her point, Lorenzo made strange moans and snuffling sounds as if struggling for breath.

Botticelli belched and climbed to his feet. "Must take a piss. Back soon." In seconds he had lumbered out the door.

"Do not leave me, Sandro! We must go!"

"Back soon," he said before slamming the door.

Look at them. I swear that wine is the scourge of us all. "My lord, please rouse yourself. The hour is late and I must be home." Gabriela shook Magnifico's arm but he didn't stir.

Get his servant. Maybe he can fix him something to bring him around.

Gabriela poked her head into the hall to address the servant standing there. "Your master sleeps but we have work still to do. Might you help me rouse him?"

"Rouse him?" said the young man in the Medici livery. "If the lord sleeps, then it is time he were abed and you scampered away home. We will assist him."

"But I know he will want to see our project through," she protested.

"Then it must wait until tomorrow, yes? I do as I always do. When the master drowns his pain in his goblet, then I am to take him up to bed, that is unless you plan to accompany him there, but since the master has little of that kind of company of late, I think not. Go home now, signorina."

Her protests were useless. While two servants helped their master out of the room and up the stairs, one downing the remains of the decanter on the way out of the room, Gabriela began rolling up the sketch. "Let us look for Sandro. He cannot be far."

Good idea.

"I am furious with you," she said, stuffing the canister into Sandro's bag and throwing it over her shoulder. "Why couldn't you not be quiet? One moment when my attention wavers and in you jump. All your talk of the future has thrown our plans off course. Had you remained silent, perhaps the sketch would be done and Sandro would either be taking me home or Magnifico would have sent an escort."

But you have the sketch and the key now. If only the wasp motif remains, you can fashion one without the artists' help. You can certainly draw and, if not, I'll help you.

"I do not want or need your help. Unless you can take me safely through the streets tonight, you are of no use to me," Gabriela said aloud.

Let's track down Botticelli.

But that turned out to be much more difficult than expected. After searching the whole bottom level of the palazzo, or at least those rooms they had access to that were not locked, they knew that the old scoundrel had left. Then a servant came across them and ordered them gone. And no, he had not seen the artist, he shouted after them as they scrambled across the garden to the stables.

"We have no choice but to take the cart and nag and hope we will arrive safely. It will be dawn within the hour." Gabriela's fear seemed to electrify her body, making her run faster than Brooke had ever experienced in her shoes.

But when they arrived at the stables, the nag and cart were gone.

"I can't believe that he's left us," Brooke exclaimed. "He must be very drunk."

"Left me, you mean. You do not even exist, remember?" Gabriela said. "And yes, he is drunk. What did I tell you?"

"Come on, let us borrow a horse."

"Steal a Medici mount? Are you mad?"

"Hey, signorina, who yer talking to?"

Gabriela swung around to find a gateman standing there, middle-aged with a mop of shaggy hair. "To one of these noble mounts," Gabriela told him.

"Yeah, but they do not want to be listening to the likes of you, do they?"

"Might I borrow one to get myself home? My escort, Signore Alessandro Filipepi, appears to have left without me."

"Botticelli? Yeah, he stumbled out of here drunk as a Venetian whore, all right, took the cart and nag with him. Think he forgets how to sit upright by the way he was toppling this way and that."

Gabriela took a step forward. "Please help me. I must get home and he's taken my only way. Please lend me a horse. The master will not mind as I came here at his bidding to do him a service."

The man pulled back, gripped his crotch, and leered. "Did him a service, did you? Used to prefer them prettier, he did. Not his usual type, are you? Likes them long and lean with long yellow hair like them kind Botticelli paints."

"In my world, they call that too much information, bozo," Brooke told him. "Now mount up a horse for us before I lose my temper."

The gateman gaped at her but soon turned at the ringing of the gate's bell. "Who goes there?" he called.

"Signore Jacopo Sistino come to retrieve my betrothed. I hear her voice in there and will fetch her home. Let me in!"

"Well, then," said the man, grinning at Gabriela. "Looks like the answer to your problem, yes?"

"No! Do not let him in, I beg of you! He is not my keeper!"

But the gateman had already released the latch.

"You *are* a Medici whore!" Jacopo accused as he flung the door back on its hinges and lunged into the stable yard. Grabbing Gabriela by the arm, he gave her wrist a painful twist, provoking Brooke to kick out, only Gabriela refused to move her limbs. "Do not deny it. I heard you say that you did him a service."

"Not that kind of service, you idiot!" Brooke yelled at him.

"Who are you calling an idiot? Have you completely lost your mind?" Jacopo's expression was half anger, half hurt.

Stay silent!

"I referred to the gateman, not you," Gabriela explained.

But then the bell rang again, this time accompanied by banging on the thick wooden slats of the main gates. "It is Signore Alessandro Filipepi. Let me in!" the voice called.

"So much excitement," muttered the gatekeeper as he lurched over to flip back the iron brace. "Hold yer horses!"

Swinging the gates open revealed a sheepish-looking Botticelli holding the nag's bridle. "Forgive me, Gabriela. I did not know what I was about until I was halfway across the piazza and then I remembered. I—" His words dropped off at the sight of Jacopo.

Jacopo looked from one to the other. "You are here with this despicable stooge? Did you remove your clothes for him while Medici watched, is that it?" He spat into the dust. "You will not be in his company again. You will return home with me, Gabriela." Turning to Botticelli he added: "And should I ever again set eyes upon you around my betrothed from this day forth, you wretched dabbler, I will set upon you with staves and break every bone in your fingers."

Sandro shoved his hands into his breeches. "We did nothing indecent," he protested.

"So you say." Jacopo dragged Gabriela through the doors toward where her old mare, Chiara, stood. First he climbed into the saddle and then ordered her up in front of him.

"But she is old and cannot take so much weight," Gabriela said, tears threatening to spill. "You will lame her!"

"Get up," Jacopo ordered. "She is but a horse and a beast of burden, not some pet to be coddled, whereas you are but a liar and a whore. I will not tolerate this foolishness a moment longer. Climb up, I say!"

But Gabriela was not to sit upright on the saddle as a woman but to lay across the horse on her stomach like a sack of potatoes. If Jacopo's intent was to humiliate her, he succeeded. Her eyes fixed on the ground, all she could do was send furious thoughts to her inner voice. *This is all your fault!*

Don't forget the sketch! Botticelli is oblivious.

Gabriela twisted her torso around and called back: "Sandro, the sketch! Your bag lies there on the ground where I dropped it! Keep it safe." And with that they began the long, laborious ride home.

"*I*s that it?"

Brooke stared across the room at Felix. "Isn't that enough?"

"What I mean is..." Felix paused to draw a deep breath. "One minute you are thrown over a horse and the next everything ends. *Pronto*—gone—which brings us back to here where we are all sitting feeling a bit lost."

Brooke rubbed a hand across her eyes. Many hours plus a good night's sleep had passed and still she remained fixed in the present. It left her reeling and feeling strangely bereft. "Lost is exactly how I feel but you, too? Everything ended because Gabriela shut me out. We were making so much progress, the two of us, but as soon as I began talking about the future to Lorenzo de' Medici, she grew furious. She blames me for Jacopo finding her, for the abysmal end to their plans—everything."

"Why did you even begin speaking about the future?" That was Enrico. "Isn't that against some statute of limitations of the league of time travelers or something? Don't look at me like that: I go to the movies, too."

Brooke shook her head. "I thought it wouldn't make any difference to Lorenzo since he was already dying, yet if something I said might protect one item of his collection—a book or a piece of art—I had to risk it. He probably didn't remember any of it the next day."

"Probably not. Lorenzo was very addled with drink and pain, but Gabriela will not forget and she's the one we need to be concerned about. I believe she needs you, Brooke. Somehow, you must return to her life and help her for the next stage of her journey."

Brooke raised her head and stared at Stephani sitting across from her holding a tiny cup of espresso. It took a moment to register how her companions seemed completely in tune with her recent past life experiences as if they had lived them, too. "Wait a minute—how do you know that? Was I talking everyone's lines like in a play last night or something?"

Enrico sat, legs crossed, with an expression of total resignation, garbed in his dapper linen pants and cable stitch pullover. Shaking his head, he said: "An apt description but not everybody got a speaking part in this little play of yours. I, for instance, have been left out of the script."

"What Enrico is attempting to say in his petulant way, Brooke," Stephani began, "is that it seems that we *are* participants in this amazing journey of yours. I was Lorenzo De' Medici in Gabriela's lifetime and Felix, Sandro Botticelli."

"What?" Brooke gasped.

"How lucky is that?" Enrico muttered. "One of us was a famous statesman and art patron, the other a master artist, whereas I was merely your father, who is now offstage somewhere."

"Oh, *amore mio*, stop." Felix grinned. "You are just jealous because I am the famous Botticelli reborn and you are—"

"Merely a bit player in this bizarre production." Enrico threw up his hands but his wry smile indicated that his pique was at least partly for show. "I keep waiting for the tailor Domenico to return but he has yet to reappear. And you are not Botticelli reborn, *tesoro*, if what Stephani says is true," Enrico pointed out.

Brooke stared at them each in turn, trying to process everything. They were completely immersed in her strange dual reality because they came back with her to the past as time shadows themselves? "Did we all roam the streets living out our past lives last night or what?"

"Absolutely not," said Enrico. "I remained in this century protecting the lot of you as you floated around the flat banging into walls and speaking in tongues."

"In other words, he barricaded the door to keep us safe," Stephani said.

When Brooke's gaze landed fully on Stephani, she could only say: "*You were Lorenzo de' Medici?*"

"Permit me to clarify." Stephani set the cup down on the coffee table and fixed Brooke with her dark eyes. "No, *I* was not Lorenzo de' Medici any more than you were Gabriela di Domenico. Lorenzo was a unique individual born into extraordinary circumstances in a fractious age influenced by countless equally extraordinary factors. Also, the gene pool that contributed to his corporal form cannot be underestimated for the way in which he developed any more than can his family, beliefs, socioeconomic status, education, and even the food he ate."

"In other words, there can never be another Lorenzo de' Medici or another Sandro Botticelli even if they share the same soul," Enrico explained.

"No, there can never be another Lorenzo de' Medici any more than there will ever be another Stephani Maria Marino or another Enrico. We are each individuals as unique as our fingerprints, partly a work of nature combined with random circumstances, and partly a product of God, however you choose to define God or even believe such exists. However, it appears some elemental aspect of me—let us call it my soul—occupied the body of Lorenzo de' Medici just as Felix's occupied Botticelli, Enrico Gabriela's father, and you Gabriela herself."

"Which means," Brooke managed to say, "that we're all interconnected around Gabriela's life. That's what drew us together in the first place."

"Correct. Past lives frequently meet up with one another across the ages, which may be why we can have such an overwhelming sense of déjà vu upon meeting certain people. Gabriela is the common denominator here," Stephani said with a nod. "She is what binds us together, we four, that and Florence itself. There must be others with whom we will no doubt encounter before this is over."

"When this is over?" Brooke repeated. "It appears to have been over the moment Gabriela shut me out."

"But you must get back and regain her trust. She needs you, of that I am convinced. Lorenzo believes that Gabriela is key in more ways than one, though I can't fathom why he holds her role as so important," Stephani said. "I sensed that the treasure he sought to protect is already safe. There was a fleeting thought I witnessed that indicated that he no longer feared his library's destruction but he feared for Gabriela."

"The famous library must have survived intact. There is the Laurentian Library, after all," Enrico reminded them.

"Perhaps but scholars believe that it is not complete, Rico. We know that the Medici pope rescued some books after the palazzo was sacked but there may have been other more valuable manuscripts secreted away by Lorenzo himself. That's what I am hoping we will discover at the end of Gabriela's journey," Stephani added.

Enrico got up and stretched. "What do we know, really, of what schemes the maestro of the Renaissance put in place when all's said and done?"

"But he claims to have made multiple plans within plans, a kind of fail-safe backup scenario like a Chinese puzzle box, if I understand correctly," Felix said. "Typical Renaissance thinking. They did love their secret codes, didn't they? Could you figure out what he was referring to, Steph?"

"Unfortunately, no." Stephani leaned back in her seat and fumbled for her cigarettes, pulling them out until she caught Enrico's eye. *"Merda!"* She withdrew her hand and scowled.

"Go out to the balcony. I even cleaned the ashtray for you," Enrico told her, pointing to the windows now open to a fresh breeze.

"Banished like so much trash. Don't you know who I am?" She tilted her chin and flashed him a smile.

"Not Magnifico, as you say yourself," Enrico reminded her, crossing his arms.

"Speaking of Lorenzo," Stephani continued while pocketing her cigarettes, "I could not grasp the whole of his complex plan. The great Medici is at the end of his days, his brain murky with pain, and most of it clouded with either drink or opium. On the rare moments when I was able to eavesdrop into his thoughts, they were so muddled that I could not follow an idea to its conclusion. The man was a genius and I have no doubt that his scheme is deviously complex but it was beyond me to understand it."

"Could you influence him in any way?" Brooke asked.

"Never! He didn't even sense my presence," Stephani assured her, getting to her feet. "His head was too blasted. I did sense his feelings and know that he looks—*looked*—upon Gabriela with almost fatherly love and complete trust. Once she proved herself over the Pazzi conspiracy, she won his loyalty absolutely."

"And Botticelli, does he trust him, too?" Felix asked.

Stephani quirked a smile. "Not very but he knows your fondness for Gabriela and trusts you won't let him or her down. Listen to me—I mean, of course, that he knows *Botticelli's* fondness for Gabriela."

"I hope that's true because what I glimpsed inside the great artist's mind last night looked like a splattered painter's palette. It's as if he couldn't keep a cohesive thought together, either, though I did get brilliant images of Madonnas and goddesses. I think the man was bit of an alcoholic as well as a genius."

"Wasn't every second person an alcoholic back then?" Enrico asked, turning to gaze out over the city.

"Probably. Had to be since the water wasn't always safe to drink," Felix acknowledged." They certainly drank wine like water. Anyway, I'd hoped I might penetrate Botticelli's mind long enough to see where he hid paintings that might still be missing, but that was useless."

"The human mind has an endless capacity to segment memories that it wants to hide or to forget or to bury deep inside itself. These are complicated people. Do not be surprised if you fail to grasp their thoughts after only a few hours inside their minds." Stephani strode toward the sliding glass doors that opened onto the balcony. "Pardon me while I head for my banishment. Lorenzo and I have that much in common."

Enrico rolled his eyes.

"But neither of you had experienced flashes of your past lives before last night?" Brooke asked, trying to keep her with them.

Stephani turned. "No, Brooke. That is the thing. It is your connection with Gabriela that has pulled us into these past lives. Maybe at some level my past soul experience with Medici explains my lifelong fascination with Renaissance art and literature, and maybe yours, Felix, and Enrico's explain your collective passions for textiles, art, and design. There is a certain sense in that, no? But that does not mean that any of us have or will share other traits or personalities with the people with whom we share our souls."

"In many ways we're different, Gabriela and I, but we have commonalities, too. I feel like we are still very bonded somehow," Brooke said.

"Your relationship with Gabriela is unique. None of us appear to have the intensity of experiences you have had. In some ways it's inexplicable, but then, so much is. We think we understand the world and try to fit our explanations into a box but much eludes us. Excuse me for one moment. Like Lorenzo, I must appease my addictions."

Brooke watched Stephani step onto the balcony and light one of her cigarettes, some of the acrid smoke leeching through the partially open door, her profile framed against the golden Duomo.

"Oh, that ghastly habit." Enrico slid the door shut. "In any case, I have yet to find myself in the life of Domenico, the tailor to the Medici," he pointed out, "and I am crushed. I wouldn't mind a chance to study his techniques, see what skills we have lost over the centuries."

Brooke cast him a sly smile. "I can help there, daddy. I have glimpsed a few interesting details when I was in the atelier."

He held up a hand. "Stop, just stop with the daddy thing. Seriously, though, Brooke, Gabriela's father appears to have disappeared."

Stephani slid the door open and poked her head through. "I sense that

Lorenzo was hiding something there, too—actually, he hides plenty, but in regards to Domenico, there were details he would not tell Gabriela."

"Like what?" Brooke asked.

"He sent him to fulfill a task and did not disclose to Gabriela the full extent of that assignment but I have no idea why." Stephani turned away to take a puff.

"Maybe the poor man is dead," Enrico suggested, "as you will be soon, Stephani, if you continue that foul habit." He waved the smoke away and slid the door shut again. "You need to discover what became of Domenico while fulfilling your past life destiny," he said to Brooke as he turned back to the room. "I'm burning with curiosity."

She gazed up at him. "Gabriela has shut me out completely. I've tried everything to return to her life, as you know. Meanwhile, I only ever got to share her life in the most important, life-changing moments, anyway, so there are huge gaps between one event and the next. I thought for certain that I'd remain with her as Jacopo rode away with her thrown over the saddle but that just might have been so humiliating a memory that she refuses to share."

"I don't believe she can just refuse you, if I understand this business correctly. You just need the right trigger," Enrico said, gazing off into the distance.

Felix joined them. "And I think I know what that may be. That dress Gabriela described to Lorenzo...I remember Gabriela's description word for word: *The velvet of the giornea as soft and glowing as sun cupped within a rosebud.* You and your passion for yellow in all its hues now makes perfect sense as does that project you did for Mario Barone in your work term all those years ago."

"Oh, my God! That 'Renaissance Monstrosity,' Mario called it," Brooke exclaimed. "I do remember. He wanted me to tear out the seams and start again but I refused and tried to hide the dress, though I eventually finished the original assignment to his exacting standards."

"Oh, yes, that evening gown. We thought it lovely, too. That was when Felix and I first came together to defend this strange little Canadian who seemed so out of her element against the design maestro. He could not deny your talent but raged against your fixation with color and certain design elements. He accused you of making costumes for a Renaissance fair, remember?"

Brooke laughed. "I remember!" And then she suddenly sobered. "I was replicating Gabriela's dress even way back then."

"And right now, in a manner of speaking, that dress plays a significant role in Gabriela and Lorenzo's strategy. It could be the trigger that will pitch you back into Gabriela's life," Felix continued.

"We kept it, you know. That's what Felix is getting at," Enrico told her. "That day when Mario screamed at you and insisted that you shred the piece and you screamed back—very Italian, that moment, by the way. Not our idea of Canadian at all. Pure passion—the two of us found a way to distract him and smuggle the piece out. It remains with us still, wrapped in tissue up in our storage facility. Until now, neither of us had any idea why we kept it."

"Now we understand. If we go there now and you interact with it again, that just might be the trigger you need," Felix finished.

"An excellent idea, but won't that pitch our little play out into the streets somewhere where we might be hit by a bus or worse?" asked Stephani, now standing beside them.

Enrico lifted his hand. "The storage facility is actually the renovated barn complex of the villa Felix and I bought up in the hills near Fiesole. Remember that outbuilding we were renovating? Finished. There we keep a copy of every one of our designs organized by year in a climate-controlled storage area. We will be as safe there as we are anywhere. Shall we go?"

Within the hour, the four of them had gathered themselves up, changed, and packed a small bag for an overnight stay.

"We had planned to take you here for a few days, Ruscello, at least before our lives tipped sideways," Felix said behind the wheel as they left the streets of Florence behind to climb into the hills. "Now you'll get to see it under slightly different circumstances."

"Won't there be people working there?" Brooke asked.

"Not now, except for our housekeeper and groundsman who we have given a few days off. This is our escape and we keep it private except for the occasional party or other festive occasion."

"It's quite delightful," Stephani remarked while admiring the passing scenery as the car left the streets of stone and began to climb.

"And I presume you've commanded a view of Florence up here, too?" Brooke was gazing through the back window wondering how much of the landscape had changed since Gabriela's time. Certainly the view of the city, one of the most photographed scenes from the surrounding area, couldn't have altered much.

"We do have a view from our pool area but otherwise this property is secluded in a grove of trees," Enrico remarked as he turned right onto a cypress-lined lane that wound down into a little dell. The buff stucco villa rose before them almost at once.

"Oh," Brooke exclaimed, studying the three-floor tiled-roof villa with its balconies and window boxes of blooming red carnations. "It's gorgeous!"

"We call it a villa but it was actually once an old farmhouse that offered us just the assembly of buildings we needed." Enrico parked in the curved gravel driveway and they all climbed out.

Staring up at the structure, Brooke inhaled deeply. "I love it already." She gazed around. "Where's the storage area?"

Felix pointed to the large fieldstone building nestled at the end of a small lane. "There. Come, I'll show you."

"Wait." Stephani placed a hand on her shoulder. "There's something you should know, Brooke. I'm guessing that the next time you enter Gabriela's life, it will be a furious headlong rush to her final chapter with no exit sign, so to speak."

Brooke turned to her. "I know. I can feel it."

"There may be no way back."

"And yet you must proceed," said Enrico. It was not a question.

"I have no choice. Either I go forward now in the company of friends or I end up stranded in my life in a stew of unfinished business all by myself. All these past life flashbacks will still continue entangling my life but I will never know a resolution if I don't continue."

Enrico and Felix flanked her, each wrapping an arm around her shoulders. "At least we'll be with you one way or another," Felix said.

She smiled at each of them in turn. "Thank you. I really appreciate everything you have done for me and continue to do, my dear friends."

"Don't sound so final, caro," Enrico said. "You will be returning to plague us another day."

She laughed but shook her head. "I hope so. Think of how dull your life might be without me. But still there's a chance that when Gabriela dies, so will I. I don't know that for certain but since we're so closely bound..."

"But not if she dies with peace in her heart," Enrico told her, "then your spirit will be free, too—both of you will. Wherever the next stage of your journey ends, be sure to let her last moments be filled with love and gratitude. That is the key."

She gazed at him, remembering how spiritual he could be at times despite the irritable exterior. "What if I am left hanging?"

"Then you must still obtain peace in those moments," Enrico said, his face suddenly so serious that she almost felt as if she spoke to another.

"Okay." Such a strange feeling standing there in the Tuscan sunlight preparing for an end that wasn't hers but which bound her lifetime so irrevocably. "Let's get this over with," Brooke said with a nod. "After all, I have another life to live."

"Pronto," Enrico said, leading her down the lane while Felix rushed ahead and typed in a code on the building's electronic lock. The mechanism beeped, Felix flicked on the lights, and the four of them stepped into a long room filled with glass-enclosed rooms.

"Oh, wow." Brooke gazed down the long corridor as each glass box was illuminated, one after the other. "This is the archive?"

"It is," Felix said over his shoulder as he strode down the hall, "but your dress we keep along with our own first efforts in the very last chamber. Wait there."

But of course Brooke had to peer into each section to marvel over the textiles, textures, and designs she spotted, each room labeled with a color photo of its contents, most modeled by the elite of the model world. She was craning to capture a better look at one of her favorite seasons—spring 2019— when Felix 's footsteps sounded on the concrete behind her.

"Brooke?"

A tremor ran through her when she saw his reflection in the glass and the sweep of yellow in his arms. "When I go this time, you won't be with me and Magnifico may be gone," she whispered. "I think I must be going on to this stage alone."

"Why do you feel that, Brooke?" her friend asked.

"I don't know." Her heart thumping, she tried to force down her rising panic. "I just fear it but that can't stop me."

Taking a deep breath, she turned.

1 2

*T*he workroom was dark when Gabriela entered early that evening. Stepping into the long room, she realized that the curtains were drawn along the courtyard-facing windows. They had once kept their workers sewing until the very last bit of sun had leeched from the sky, straining their eyes in the half-light to finish a seam or sew a hem or needle a few remaining pearls onto an embroidered bodice for some important client. Once they had been far too busy to waste a single moment and yet now their workshop lay empty.

When she had emerged from the room where she was required to spend her day in Bible study, she found the house empty. Even Maria was gone. She tried to remember if Jacopo had mentioned an appointment with an important client or some other explanation that would shut the shop down. By necessity, he arranged such meetings in secrecy now. Even if he had such an assignation, it did not explain Maria's absence. Had he gone to a noble's house to fit a man's apparel and taken her with him? Certainly the woman had assumed more authority in their household over the years.

As a young girl Gabriela had attended the city's noblewomen in the privacy of their quarters. Women who had preferred a female to fit them were happy that her father could afford that service but now their clients were more reluctant to have visits under any circumstances. Clarice de' Medici had once used her services exclusively but that was long ago before that lady had died and the great Medici had fallen. Fallen, yes, but not forsaken, at least not by her. Gabriela would enact the instructions of the late Lorenzo the Magnificent no matter how long it took her or at what cost.

She shook herself from her reverie. Enough time wasted. She could not squander this opportunity to be alone in her one remaining sanctuary.

Gabriela scanned the massive tables where lengths of silk and velvet were spread in jewel-colored sweeps awaiting the first cut or the continuation of some fine detail upon the rich fabric. These were once her paints, her tools, and she resisted the urge to stroke them in passing lest she snag a pin or worse.

Lighting a lantern, she carried it past the tables, averting her eyes from the dress forms that stood around the room in various states of undress. They always seemed to watch her reproachfully and, in the twilight, cast distorted shadows that had once frightened her as a child. Perhaps even still…

But she was no longer a child, she reminded herself. In the Florentine republic few knew the truth: that she, Gabriela di Domenico, a mere woman, had once been the designer of the most fabulous gowns for which her father's house had become famous. Her—not her father, not their then-assistant, Jacopo—but her, a woman daring to take the work of God into her own hands to create exquisite designs for the Florence nobility, designs that had gathered such fame that wealthy houses as far away as Rome had requested their artistry. Yet, in these days when such luxury was viewed as sinful, her involvement would only draw further wrath upon their heads and must remain secret, as must another, much darker confidence.

If Florence knew the truth, the business would be ruined, the great Medici might be further sullied, and Gabriela herself sent to a convent or much, much worse. She could not bear to imagine what cruel humiliation might be inflicted upon her should the secret be exposed. Had she not endured enough once forced to marry Jacopo?

Women were put on earth for but one role. How many times had she heard that? She was to bear children and to serve men and God, at times the two seeming one and the same: marry, bear children, obey, obey. But Gabriela was not born to obey but to create. Why else would she have been given this gift—to transform a bolt of cloth into something extraordinary, something that served as a tribute to God since all the glorious details were crafted in His name? As for having a child, not with Jacopo, she prayed. Never that. There were tricks she wielded, but if ever he should discover her ploys…

But enough of that. What she delighted most in was imagining God's creatures—the birds, the flowers, the insects—and bringing them alive on a sleeve or a hem. The craftspeople had breathed life into her sketches, a great design became reality, and beauty sang its song in her art. How could this be sinful?

She strode down the long room toward the secret door, driven by her determination to see this thing through. Time was running out. The great Lorenzo de' Medici had made but one request of her before he died, a simple one on the surface, but one she knew bore unknown repercussions for all involved. He knew it might take years to bring into fruition but implored her to wait, if necessary, and wait she had. Now could not be a worse time to put his request into action. Nevertheless, a promise made must be honored, especially to the dead.

Fingering the key in her purse at her waist, she imagined the small flat object slipping into the seam in such a way as to be unnoticeable amid the velvets and silks. It would be transported as requested and her reward duly accepted, a reward she was only too eager to receive considering that there was no other way she could ever obtain the largesse otherwise.

Though her father had been successful and his coffers had swelled accordingly, they had never been permitted to wear the clothes they crafted even when they could afford them, *especially* when they could afford them. The sumptuary laws made that clear: beautiful clothes were for noble citizens only and then for special occasions with the details carefully regulated—that is, before the friar Savonarola preached that all such luxuries were sin incarnate. Now people hid their beautiful clothes in shame. But Gabriela would enact more than one defiance before this game was over.

The edges of the door blended seamlessly with the end wall, expertly camouflaged by the playful painting Fili had worked of the Florentine citizens garbed in Domenico finery before he had left the city. She followed the line of a full-skirted gamurra with her finger until she heard the mechanism spring loose.

Stepping into the darkened room, she latched the door behind her and set the lantern on the table. Her eyes were drawn immediately to the center of the floor. There, glowing in the lamplight, stood the dress on its form just as she had left it, a vision in solitary glory on a mannequin crafted exactly to her size —and originally Clarice and Lorenzo de' Medici's eldest daughter, Lucrezia, by happenstance and ingenuity. That noble lady would never wear this piece now. If Savonarola had his way, no one would.

Here was her art, a multilayered column of the finest gold-threaded lemon-colored embroidered velvet overlaying a soft silk camicia the color of molten pearls. How her heart sang when she had first touched that fabric, enchanted by the way in which the colors changed every time she lifted the lengths this way and that—from lemon to deepest gold, a trick of the weaver's art where two colors of silk were napped to fool the light. When worn, the piece would shimmer and glow as if touched by a nymph or some other marvelous mythological creature who altered matter with a sweep of its hand.

Let Fili and Sandro work their magic on flat surfaces with their paint. Her alchemy moved with the body, blew with the wind, danced in the nuances of light and shadow. Living art, she had teased them. "Can you make your creations move?" she called out to her betrothed one afternoon as he stood painting in his studio.

"I cannot, my love!" he had laughed over his shoulder, his brush held aloft, but in truth Filippino, like Sandro, were such masters of their art that it was as though his figures breathed from the wood they were painted upon. His work caused her breath to still and her heart to flutter. Or maybe that had been his doing...

Gabriela smiled at the memory as she untied her brown work dress and let it drop to the floor. These were the moments she treasured most. When she donned the dress, she was a bride in her heart even if such a union would never occur. If Fili knew that she had been forced to wed, would it make her less desirable in his eyes? She had no choice, as did most women, but she was prepared to live in sin if he'd have her.

Carefully lifting the lemon-gold giornea from the mannequin, she dropped it over her head and allowed it to flow down over her cotton chemise. As always, it fit perfectly, causing her to sigh as her hands smoothed over the raised velvet pattern.

Her father would scold her if he were to catch her doing this, but since she had not heard from him in years, she doubted that would ever happen. How she'd love to hear his voice once again, no matter what the reason. He would say that to wear this gown even for a moment was like tempting the Fates. It didn't matter if she was the one to fashion it into existence or that she had once prayed it might even become her own wedding gown. Here was her version of sacred.

Gently, she picked up one of the sleeves from the pair lying on the table and slipped her left arm inside, holding it to her shoulder by the ribbon ties. Here was her true masterpiece, every motif crafted to her, Sandro's, and the Magnificent's specifications before he had drawn his last breath. Every image told a story—her story as well as the secret the Medici requested embedded amid the creatures of garden and field. The great Lorenzo had caught the meaning when he had first studied Sandro's sketch years before but had only nodded and smiled. He had so enjoyed her little puzzles as he had told her often enough. She was the sparrow, always the sparrow.

As long as the sparrow fulfilled her obligations, the dress and all else would be hers. Whether she would risk wearing it was another story and one not destined to be told within the walls of the republic. Their deal had been sealed years ago, though it would take much longer for her to enact now that the Medici power had bled from the streets of Florence. Yet she prayed that there were those still willing to enable the plan.

Holding the ribbon, her gaze swung toward the secret compartment where the sketch lay hidden. Sandro's promise of that painting for their wedding gift had thrilled Fili, too, even though Sandro warned that the portrait might take years to complete given his current work schedule. All that was needed was patience, apparently, patience and great care that they could play this game of intrigue in a city fraught with dangerous secrets. She could only hope that she was up to the challenge.

A sharp sound shattered her reverie. Swinging around, she stared at the front wall. It was all that she could do to keep from crying out. Was that Jacopo? She slipped off the sleeve and picked up the lantern, holding it high as she tiptoed toward the door, keeping the gamurra raised in one hand.

She thought only to open the door a crack and check the workroom but something cautioned her to freeze. Voices calling out. Someone stifling a sharp cry while another shouted her name. What was happening? And then she knew: they had been found out, their secret discovered. Now the rabble came to raze their house to the ground.

She swung away, torn between staying or escaping with what she alone could salvage but, in truth, there was no choice to be made. All had been agreed in advance: if ever the day came and their secret exposed, she was to run, run as far as she could, escape Florence forever. She had promised, more a pact than a decision, and one to which she was bound.

Her heart galloping, she swiftly stepped out of the gown and bundled up every precious piece of the fabric into an old cloth before donning her own clothes. The banging shook the walls. She did not have the time to cover the dress properly. With her head bare and her identity revealed to all who would look closely, she slipped across the room to another secret door that would take her down a set of stairs to a back lane, her parcel held like a limp body in her arms. At the last minute, she snatched a scrap of fabric from the floor and threw it over her head.

As her feet scuffed down the stone steps, she could not believe what she was doing, could not believe that she might never see her home again, that she would escape her beloved city that very night. Though the price of her failure was great, the price of her success was equally so.

In the dark lane between the buildings, she gripped her bundle like a huge swaddled child before stepping into a main road. Startled, she was immediately swept into a stream of moving bodies heading in the direction of the city center. With their torches and lanterns held aloft, it was as if a seething human tide pushed her forward.

They all carried something, she realized—parcels, paintings, even fistfuls of jewelry—and they were not peasants but noblemen. She struggled to break free, to turn and run toward the Porta al Prato as planned, but no, the crowd held her tight. Men, they were all men.

"What is that you carry, woman?" called the man to her right. "Do you bring a trifle of luxury to feed the flames?"

"Flames?" she cried. "I know nothing of flames! I desire only to deliver this dress to my mistress. She awaits!"

If ever the streets of Florence burn...

But already the man had been swallowed up by other bodies surging in from neighboring streets as the crowd pushed their heaving force into the Piazza della Signoria.

Even from a distance, she could feel the heat and smell the smoke but Gabriela was not prepared for the sight that awaited. A massive bonfire burned like the jaws of hell in the center of the piazza sending boiling smoke and licks of flame far into the night. Citizens could be seen throwing objects into the fire—paintings, dresses, books!

Somebody shoved her forward. A friar in dark robes stepped toward her. "Feed the flames in the name of God!" he cried, pointing to her bundle. She looked down as a single sleeve loosened from her arms and hung gleaming naked in the firelight.

13

"*G*ive it over, child. God awaits your sacrifice." The friar extended a sooty hand.

Gabriela backed away. "It is not mine to give." With that she turned and spun into the crowd, the faces rising before her seeming crazed, almost demonic, as they brought their treasures to feed the flames.

Halfway across the piazza, she stopped, clutching her bundle closer. She must find Sandro. When the streets of Florence burned, he was to meet her in his studio, that had been the promise made to Medici long ago. Had she misjudged the signs? First the great Lorenzo de' Medici had died and then soon after the throng had razed his palazzo, stealing everything not already hidden and exiling the remaining family. Should she have left then? But she couldn't find Sandro, and Jacopo kept her on too tight a rein to escape.

Now she questioned her every thought. Imprisoned in her home, her father lost to her, had she the choice, she would have chosen the life of a convent rather than to be wife to Jacopo. Better to be a servant to God than slave to a man. Still, she refused to forsake her promise. Not given lightly, equally it would not be broken lightly. If she could not find Sandro, then she must continue on alone.

It was by happenstance that she glimpsed a firelit face in the crowd, one she knew too intimately—Jacopo himself, his arms filled with dresses, *her* dresses, the samples she had housed in the studio. They had once served to show customers her designs, back in the days when she was allowed to create.

And the gold glinting between his fingers, she recognized that, too—the necklace her father had given her mother long ago. At his feet, toppled a stack of books. He was burning her work, her father's, and her library! Bastard! She'd rip them right from his hands, force him to turn away from the flames with her creations—

Stop, Gabriela! Don't be crazy. He'll make you to burn the yellow dress in your arms and the sleeves with it!

Gabriela froze. Voice. It had been years since she'd heard her last but here she was again. *Brooke?*

Gather your wits and let's follow through on your promise to Lorenzo. We'll try Botticelli's studio first and then go to Fiesole ourselves, if we have to. First, wrap up the dress. Hold it as if it's a baby and that you're off to find a nurse.

"I forget myself, as if I lost my soul for a time." Gabriela laughed at her little joke as she wrapped the yellow dress into a tighter bundle. "Move aside," she called out to the crowd. "My baby is sick and I must find help!"

The crazed-looking faces took one look at her arms before turning their attention back to the huge flaming creature burning in the center of the piazza. It held sway on everyone as the friar called out for more sacrifices as if to appease the hunger of some ancient monster. Children didn't matter, babies didn't matter. Women certainly didn't matter.

Gabriela ran down one of the side streets, swimming against the tide toward her home, Brooke talking away inside her head.

I was afraid I'd never get back to you in time. It was like you were locked away from me.

"I was locked away from even myself," Gabriela explained aloud, every passerby probably assuming that she spoke to her babe. Occasionally, she brought the supposed child over her shoulder and patted its back. "Jacopo and the priests locked me in a room where I was to read the Bible and pass certain tests each day in order to prove I wasn't possessed. Then in the evenings, Jacopo attempted to get me pregnant as a further cure for my willfulness. I despise him! He has assumed control of the business and our prosperity has dwindled as a result. No word from Father after all these years." She seemed to stumble over her words. "And Fili, I wrote to him so many times but I believe my letters were intercepted for I have never had a reply. We can never marry now that Jacopo has claimed me as his own."

Gabriela, you are not a thing for someone else to take. Let him think he owns you all he wants. It will make no difference if you're not around for him to own. Don't tell me that you've spent all these years locked away without hope?

"The only thing that kept me alive was my secret room. I escaped every chance I got. Sometimes when Jacopo fell into a drunken slumber or remained out too late or was in bed with Maria, I would sneak to my secret room. This dress is all that remains of me."

That bastard's such a hypocrite. But that dress reminds you who you are. Let's find Botticelli.

That turned out to be easier than expected. They found the door of the painter's studio hanging broken on its hinges while, inside, Sandro himself perched on a stool drinking himself into a stupor. Around him, boards had been ripped from the walls or torn up from the floors.

"Gabriela!" Seeing her, he lurched up from his seat. "Is it truly you?"

"Sandro!" She was so excited to see him again that for a moment she didn't notice the state of the studio—or him. Then it struck her. "What has happened here?"

"They came to the door, the friar's holy child soldiers, demanding I give them something to burn in the name of God so I dug up all the paintings I had hidden. I have given them my paintings," he sobbed, "told them to burn the pagan goddesses in order to save my soul. Gone, they are all gone." He wiped his eyes on his sleeve.

"Sandro, no!"

"Seriously? How could you bear to do it?" Brooke demanded. "I'd read somewhere that they thought you might have burned some of your own art in Savonarola's flames but I didn't believe it until now."

Sandro crossed himself. "To save my soul, I said. Gabriela, you are still possessed by this demon? I will not address her. Tell her to be silent."

"Speak to me, then," Gabriela told him, "but she is no demon. Now tell me, did you give them my portrait, too?"

Botticelli gave her a sly grin, revealing enough of the man she used to be to give her hope. "Never. I have kept my promise and hidden it well inside our Ognissanti."

"You hid it inside the church?" Gabriela exclaimed. "Brilliant! Now you must keep your other promise to Magnifico and help me escape into the hills."

A look of fear crossed his face. "They are all gone, Gabriela, the Medici and all their books destroyed. The pope, he rescued some, I hear, but not all. It is too late."

That infuriated her. "It is not too late, Sandro. What has become of you? My own father gave his life to smuggle the Medici treasure out of Florence and now we must play our part to ensure that it remains in the right hands. It is our vow. The knowledge of the world may depend upon it."

"And this is the perfect opportunity tonight when Florence's attention is fixed on staging Savonarola's Bonfire of the Vanities," Brooke added before Gabriela cut her off.

"What I mean to say is that the timing could not be better," Gabriela continued. "The entire city is in the Piazza della Signoria tonight, even my useless husband, giving us a chance to escape undetected."

"But if they catch me, Savonarola may withdraw his promise to grant me more church commissions. I cannot risk it." The artist took another swig from the bottle before burying his face in his paint-stained hands. "I am sorry, Gabriela, but I cannot go."

Gabriela wrenched the bottle from his hands and emptied it onto the floor. "If that's all you care about, your soul is already corrupt, Sandro. Get up."

"Go away," he sniveled.

"So you have bargained with the devil yourself, Botticelli, is that it?" Brooke burst out. "You would forsake your patron and your friend here for the power-hungry little upstart who will be hung himself soon enough?"

Botticelli looked up, aghast. "He will be hung? Who would hang a priest?"

"The pope himself will see that Savonarola comes to a bad end because he becomes too powerful, too full of himself," Brooke said. "Besides, the citizens will get tired of him soon enough. This is the city of art and design. How long do you think Florence will allow what made it prosperous—what it loves—to be shamed and destroyed? You can't keep the human spirit down for long. What's happened to yours?"

"So get up and let us go!" Gabriela tugged the artist by the arm. "Quick, where is your mount?"

As if in answer, a whinny sounded from the far end of the room. Gabriela peered into the shadows until she could pick up the shape of a horse and two-wheeled trap. "You brought another cart?"

"I had planned to bring all my paintings back to the cottage I share with my brother but the friar's soldiers accosted me first so I gave them all away."

"No matter," Gabriela told him. "It will do. We are going to Fiesole where I am to be delivered to a Franciscan monastery. Is that not true? Did you know if the same abbot, the friend to the Medici, lives there still?"

"I do not know, Gabriela," the artist said, stumbling after her, but if you go and Jacopo comes after, you will be shamed in the streets and ruined."

"If I stay I will be ruined, too. Come, Sandro. When did you become so fearful of everything? I remember how you once brimmed with excitement and inspiration and hardly recognize this broken man afraid of everything and believing every word told to him."

"Broken?" protested Botticelli, climbing up into the trap beside Gabriela.

"Yes, broken. I have recently been broken, too, and can recognize it in another. Now, if anyone accosts us, say that I am your daughter and that you are delivering me to a convent. Ready?"

"This is mad," protested the artist, but he clicked at the horse, which trotted through the doors for the street. "I heard that you were forced to wed that useless Jacopo."

"I was, I did, and now I am escaping."

They traveled for hours, riding into the sunrise along a trail that wound into the hills, Gabriela now taking over the reins while Sandro slumbered. Handfuls of people had passed them heading into Florence during the night but nobody bothered with them other than to exchange remarks.

Eventually, Sandro roused, reclaiming the reins while muttering about how his head ached and his mouth tasted like a stable floor.

"Fetch me water from the flask in my bag," he asked. "I think my head will burst off my shoulders."

Gabriela reached into his leather satchel, surprised to find a loaf of sliced bread and cheese there as well as the flask. Soon she was breaking her fast when a monk called out to them from the path.

"Hail, there," called the brown-robed friar. "Did you attend the bonfire, good folks?"

"Yes," Botticelli said, swallowing his own last bite of cheese before wiping his mouth on his sleeve. "We watched the citizens feed the flames with their baubles."

"Ah, good. We wished to have seen such a holy spectacle but will go to hear Savonarola speak this very day. Good day to you." And off he went.

"Holy spectacle?" said Brooke aloud. "Is there such thing as a 'holy spectacle'? Sounds like an oxymoron to me."

"Is that you, Gabriela, or that creature that lives inside you that speaks?"

"That was Brooke," Gabriela said, flicking crumbs off her cloak.

"Pray tell her to remain silent for I cannot comprehend a single word she speaks."

Gabriela only sighed and folded her hands onto the babe in her lap. Then she had the idea to bundle up the silks into one of Sandro's bags, thinking that made a far better receptacle. The gown would be creased and possibly stained even in its wrapping but it seemed preferable to keeping it in a loose bundle that always risked breaking free.

It was not difficult to learn of where the monastery was located as it was considered a prime institution in the surrounding countryside. The San

Francesco Monastery rose in a cluster of stone buildings on the crest of the hill overlooking Florence and seemed at once both welcoming and austere.

"I much prefer the Franciscans to the Dominicans," Botticelli whispered, gazing up at the structure, "but neither will welcome a sinner like me and a woman not at all. You must remain outside the gates while I seek out the abbot."

"Is there a code word or a certain sentence you are to speak when you meet him?" Gabriela asked.

"The Magnifico said only that I was to introduce myself and evoke his name, for the Medici were once patrons of the establishment and gave money for its chapel."

"As good an opening as any," Brooke remarked.

Sandro shot her a quick glance before climbing out of the trap. "Wait here. I trust I will not be long."

Gabriela climbed off the cart to stretch her legs and to give the horse a chance to graze on the grass that grew around the gates. Overhead the sun was blazing and she sought out shade beneath a tree, careful to keep the satchel close by.

Away from the fractious energy of the city where the air blew sweet and clear, a glimmer of hope returned. Perhaps she would find Fili, rediscover her father, and even find some measure of happiness once again. Happiness once experienced becomes a beacon the heart seeks again and again. In this haze of remembered joy, she dozed off and even Brooke's inner chatter fell silent.

"Wake up! We must be away!"

Gabriela jolted upward, finding herself spread out on the grass, resting her head on the satchel. "What is happening?"

"It was a mistake to come here," Sandro hissed. "Our enemies awaited our arrival and took me captive! I broke free only with the help of one of the friars. The Abbot Fiscoli is dead and his replacement no friend of the Medici. Run, I say!"

She must have slept for hours and practically stumbled in slumber as she gazed around for Sandro's horse. But the beast had wandered off, leaving the buggy abandoned in the grass.

Sandro was calling out for the animal when a lone friar came bolting out through the gates.

"Gabriela di Domenico," he called.

"Yes, it is I."

"I bring you a message. Seek shelter at the Convent di San Francesco. Go west. Quickly."

Gabriela did not know if it was a trick but she forced herself to remain still as the young man came running up. "The convent," he whispered, taking her hand and fixing her with an earnest gaze. "The late abbot said I was to give you this message but only to you. Say the words to the abbess only," and he added in Latin: *"Ego adducere clavis ad Scriptorium."*

"I bring the key to the scriptorium?"

"Go!" the young monk insisted. "Wait for no one and go alone but go now." He was pointing to the west where the sun hung low in the sky.

In a moment, he had turned, ducking behind some hedges as five tonsured men burst through the gates. She saw them before they noticed her. Seconds later, she had flung her hood over her head and dove into the bushes, the satchel flung over her shoulder.

Behind her she heard the men calling to Sandro. Just for a moment she turned to see him galloping away on his horse as the men barreled after him. Then she ran.

14

She had no idea which way to head. Since west was her only instruction, she followed the setting sun and could only hope that Sandro escaped unharmed. But why should he not? It was her they wanted, or rather her clues. The monks did not follow. Brooke believed it was because they wrongly assumed that the painter of naughty women must be the true target rather than her.

Ego adducere clavis ad Scriptorium.

For all the years that she had worked on this secret with the great Medici, seldom had she given thought to that key once she had hidden it, as promised. But if the motifs themselves were clues, what purpose did the actual clavis perform? She had long ago decided not to strive to understand a plan for which she lacked all the components. For now, her path was clear: find the convent.

But as was the case throughout much of the region, there were multiple convents and monasteries with signposts pointing this way and that. They were but one acceptable refuge against the world for men and the only option other than marriage and motherhood for women. Many wealthy families dispatched their youngest daughters to the convents when the resources for dowries ran dry. Some patriarchs would rather consign a daughter to the church than fix her up with a bad marriage, "bad" meaning a match that might besmirch the family name. A daughter's happiness was never a factor. Of course, a loving father wished his daughter to be well fed and tended at least.

Much like a horse or the family dog.

Gabriela had almost forgotten that Brooke was there. "Yes, in truth."

But how did these convents survive when they had so many mouths to feed?

"They do not come free," Gabriela explained. "Families must provide a tithe and sometimes the better the tithe, the better the treatment. Not all girls must take the veil, either. Some live on in comfortable simplicity, though they must learn to read and work to assist the convent, too."

Like a hotel or boarding school?

"I do not quite catch your meaning but probably. I am only now realizing how lucky I was to be reared by a family who needed my skills and to have fallen under the patronage of a man like Magnifico, who nurtured all that made me unique," she said aloud. "Only now," she admitted, "it leaves me realizing how unprepared am I for the average life."

She plodded on, the two of them silent but for an occasional exchange of ideas. Every time they heard or saw company on the road ahead, Gabriela would dive for the bushes, hiding there until they had passed.

What are you afraid of?

"Everything."

As darkness fell, her fear increased, Brooke keeping her company. At last, just as the last bit of sun leeched from the sky, a signpost appeared pointing to the Convento di San Francesco.

"This must be it," Gabriela said. "At last. I thought I could not walk another step."

By now her feet ached and the great open spaces of the land around her brought another kind of uneasiness. Her life had been spent hemmed in by buildings, the press of bodies, noise, and demands of every kind. Open spaces, trees, and a road rising ahead required getting used to. In ways it was freeing, in others terrifying. Suddenly she had to rely totally on her own resources. The occasional signpost was no match for the constant questioning that filled in all those empty spaces in her mind. Only in her case, she had Brooke to fill the void.

Maybe in the end we're all meant to find our own way and it's much harder when our mind is cluttered with so much noise.

And then Gabriela fixed on the glow of lanterns through the trees ahead and hardly paid her inner voice any mind. First she saw the roof of a stone church edged against the sky and, as she drew closer, the cluster of the surrounding buildings lit by candlelight within. Soon she was running across the grass toward the door on the side of the church that she knew must lead to the convent. Banging on the door, her heart pounding equally loudly, she waited and waited but no one came.

High above, the walls darkened in the shadows to create a formidable barrier. Only the light in the lantern hanging by the door and the painting of the Virgin captured in a niche above it gave any hint of welcome.

Walls in this century always look like fortresses, Brooke remarked.

"Because we have much to protect ourselves from, do we not?" And then, after a moment, they heard the sound of singing coming from within. "They are at vespers," Gabriela said. "We must wait."

I am not Catholic so I don't understand these things.

"Vespers is an evening prayer. Do you not attend church?"

No, actually.

"You are a heathen. In any case, we must wait."

And wait they did until finally the door creaked open and there stood a nun clothed in a dark brown habit.

"Please, sister, I have an urgent message for the abbess," Gabriela told her. "It is important."

The nun nodded but said nothing. Moments later, she was led through a narrow whitewashed corridor punctuated by crosses at intervals and with doors opening off to either side. She was led into a little lamp-lit room lined with books with a simple desk and two wooden chairs against the walls. "Stay here until Abbess Cosimato can see you," the sister whispered.

Abbess Cosimato. Who was she and how was she involved in Magnifico's scheme?

Gabriela studied the room, simple yet comfortable with many books— books! It had been so long since she had been permitted to touch anything but the same folio of psalms and a Bible that she longed to investigate further. These books lay on slanted shelves, three to a shelf, a total of ten altogether.

Leaning forward, she studied the one closest to her, thrilled to see the leather-bound volume open on an illuminated page curling with gold leaf amid exquisitely contrived figures of saints holding up their palms in blessing. All of them were female, she realized—Saint Clare of Assisi, the first follower of Saint Francis of Assisi, being the largest and most central figure.

"I see that you are curious," said a voice behind her. "Here we celebrate God's glory in a multitude of ways, all using the gifts which He bestowed upon us."

Turning, Gabriela met an older woman's gaze—frank, direct, unflinching, not at all what she expected. "Abbess?" She bowed her head and curtsied.

The abbess's face was lined with the map of her years and yet her eyes

THE SPIRIT IN THE FOLD

were quick and lively. The sister smiled. "It is my name here within these walls. And you are?"

"Gabriela di Domenico, Mother, from Florence and I bring you a message from Lorenzo de' Medici: *Ego adducere clavis ad Scriptorium.*"

The eyebrows arched as the abbess brought her hands together. "God be praised! I thought you would never arrive, child." She took Gabriela's hands in hers and squeezed them warmly. "I have waited for your arrival for many seasons. I feared that you had come to harm."

"You have been expecting me?" Already her heart was singing.

"I have," the abbess said with a smile. "Once we heard that the Medici had fallen, we feared that all of his supporters might fall with him, especially any creators of fine works of art, clothing, and authors of all kinds. We have had word of Friar Savonarola's bonfire. You are here now. Follow me. We must waste no more time."

"I would have come sooner if I could have got away." But that sounded like a weak excuse to her now. Her broken spirit had plunged her into some kind of deadness of the soul that had left her flailing.

You were depressed. Give yourself a break.

What does that even mean? Gabriela hurried after the nun as she strode through corridors, through doors and passageways, weaving deeper into the cluster of buildings. Sometimes another nun or novice would approach the abbess, which prompted Abbess Cosimato to stop long enough to dispense instructions, pose questions of the sister, and sometimes even take the woman's hand or give her an encouraging smile before moving on.

It's as if she really is a sister, Brooke said.

"We are a school, a library, and even house workshops as well as a sanctuary of prayer and reflection for our sisters and charges, all to apply minds, hearts, and skills in the name of God," the abbess said as they hurried along. "The workrooms are closed for the night as all but the lay sisters are at prayer but there is one room I must show you."

Pausing at a door at the end of a long corridor, Abbess Cosimato lit a lantern, took a key from the chatelaine at her waist, and entered a long room. Raising the lantern, she drew the light along the work benches, catching silks and satins, cottons and velvets, in every imaginable hue spread upon the tables in various stages of completion.

"Behold, our atelier. We design and work the vestments and altar cloths for churches throughout the land, our efforts providing our sisters with food and clothing. Though we receive payment from the families of our charges and patrons, we believe that God rewards those that tend to their own needs."

Gabriela fingered a swath of crimson silk embroidered with flowers and birds, her heart beating so fiercely she thought it might burst. "You create beauty?"

"Yes, that is what we strive to do always. Beauty warms the heart and gives us courage. Beauty is color touched with light. Beauty is a gift from God."

"May I show you something?"

"Of course."

Gabriela slowly withdrew the bundle from her bag, unfolded the hopsacking that surrounded it, letting it drop to the floor. Holding up first one sleeve, then the other, and placing both carefully on the table, she lifted the giornea up next and stared in pleasure as the lamplight flickered lemon-gold color across the glowing lengths.

The abbess pressed a hand to her lips. "Oh, blessed wonder! Who's work is this?"

"Mine," she replied, trying hard to keep the pride from her voice and failing. "It was to be my wedding dress. The sleeves were contrived by the artist they call Botticelli, the great Magnifico himself, and me working together and they hold a deeper secret. It is why I am here. Or so I believe."

Mother Superior nodded. "I understand now why Lorenzo sent you to me. This dress is part of the reason why you are here, the Medici secret another. You say that it is to be your wedding dress?"

"Was to be, Mother. I am already wed but not to the man I gave my heart to. I escaped my husband, who would not permit me to work my art now that my father is gone. My heart's betrothed is a painter but I am no longer free."

Why did the abbess refer to Medici as Lorenzo? Brooke asked.

Gabriela had wondered the same thing. "Did you know Magnifico, Mother?"

The woman gave a little smile. "I did. It may surprise you to know that I have not always been a nun. Come, fold away all that beauty, and we will proceed to the scriptorium."

Gabriela was soon following behind the abbess, holding her dress in her arms like a precious child. They crossed the cloisters toward a building tucked in a far corner with shuttered windows opening onto the garden. "You say that you were not always a nun, Mother?" She hurried after her.

"Not always, no. I was once married to a wealthy noble in Florence, and when he died, I took the veil. I expected to confront a life of deprivation but was surprised to learn how one can replace one kind of richness for quite another. Here we are."

The abbess unlocked another door, this one opening to a long, narrow room lit by two large candelabra illuminating shelves of books along the interior wall and slanted desks positioned along the long bank of shuttered windows. A trestle table ran down the middle. One sister could be seen hard at work bent over what looked to be a sheet of vellum.

"Sister Maria Lionella, I have warned you not to strain your eyes at night. Give them a rest. God will not be pleased if you should damage the gift He has given you."

The young nun turned as if caught in some guilty act and jumped to her feet to begin tidying the work area. "I am sorry, Mother. Pray forgive me but I wanted only to finish Saint John's robe. I did not like the way in which the fabric fell about his feet so I hoped to repair it."

"It is safe to say that the good saint will wait until morning for you to adjust his clothing. Leave us now." The abbess smiled as the young sister scuttled away. "She is very talented but her ardor concerns me at times. She would work all day and night if I permitted it," she added after she had left.

"I understand her passion," Gabriela said, gazing down the long room. "To strive at what you love is such a joy. I did not realize that the convent would have its own scriptorium."

"Our sisters are artists and scribes as well as students. This convent must be our sanctuary of learning for women in a world that does not always treasure such. There is little enough retreats available for our gender. No sister is barred from the library or the scriptorium, though we do adhere to certain rules. Or attempt to."

"When my friend and I first came to the monastery down the road, a band of monks chased Sandro, I believe with the intent to capture me and the secret I carry. I thought that was where we were to go at first but a young monk sent us here," Gabriela explained.

"That was to be your first stop. The late abbot was a good man, may God rest his soul, and kept me informed of the events of the world. He would have put a plan in place in the event of his demise just as I have done. He knew his likely predecessor had been infiltrated by Savonarola's convictions. I am surprised that the new abbot would go so far as to attempt to capture you, but then, I should not be so shocked. The struggle between Savonarola and Lorenzo de' Medici is legendary. It is as much a battle of the wills as it is about a battle of convictions. Now," she said, turning to Gabriela with a smile, "*Ego adducere clavis ad Scriptorium. Do you have the key?"

Gabriela plunged her hand into her bodice where she'd hidden the key.

The abbess took the filigreed object, worked as it was in the shape of a trefoil, and held it up to the light. "So like Lorenzo to fashion his key so. Now, where do we apply it?"

Gabriela stared. "But I thought that you would know, Mother."

15

"*D*id he not say?" The abbess gazed at Gabriela, her eyebrows forming a perfect arch under her wimple.

"No. He helped design the sleeves and then gave me the key. Is there not something on which we can try it, perhaps a chest of some sort?"

"There is no casket or chest in this facility that I cannot open and none to have arrived from Lorenzo de' Medici. Bring out the dress again. Let us study those sleeves together."

They spread the sleeves on a long table in the center of the scriptorium.

"Every motif is part of the puzzle," Gabriela explained. "I understand the meaning of many elements well enough but not how the whole come together."

"How do you read it thus far?" the abbess asked, standing back.

Gabriela pointed to the sparrow. "The Medici crests speak for themselves but the sparrow is me, the symbol of humility, which I am sad to say I do not possess. It was Magnifico's and my little joke. The bee is industry, the wasp I aways believed stood for the Vespuccis, but what role they play in this, I do not know. The red carnation depicts love, where I hope Magnifico referred to my love for Fili but who knows there, either? The maestro would not say. The dandelion is the symbol for innocence. Then, on the left under-sleeve, he requested that I work a lily for the virgin, a peach for virtue and honor, and a key much like the one he entrusted me here."

"And the right sleeve?" the abbess prompted.

"Since the left sleeve is by decree the main display, I have not considered the right overmuch, though I did enjoy working those motifs, the tower in particular."

"The tower," the abbess mused. "And a very indistinguishable tower it is, too."

They gazed down at the brown crenellated watchtower worked in thick brown silk gleaming in the candlelight. "Ordinary in every way since there is one much like it attached to every church, civic or boundary wall, or villa in the land. Magnifico did not wish me to apply any other adornment."

"Making it appear exceedingly common and yet—" the abbess paused, drawing a line with her finger left and right "—perhaps not so common when flanked by this flower and that particular blossom."

Gabriela stared at the small purple flower into which she had beaded a bright yellow stamen. "The crocus?"

"No ordinary crocus but one from which the spice called saffron is harvested. Only one area that I know of in this region attempts to grow it, on an estate not but twenty miles from here. On one side of the road you see a field of crocus, on the other side an orchard of peaches, for which that white flower is meant to be its blossom, correct?" She pointed to the cluster of white flowers flanking the tower.

For a moment Gabriela held her breath. "Correct."

"And there stands the crenellated tower," the sister said, pointing.

"Do you know this place?" Gabriela asked.

"I believe so. Actually, the tower is inside a hamlet where the workers who till the land for the family live. The villa is nearby. I visited it long ago to attend a wedding of the owner of the estate to the youngest daughter of Piero Vespucci. There is a small chapel there."

"The Vespucci, whose emblem is the wasp, are family friends of the Medici? I knew them once."

"Just so."

"And Magnifico knew that you would recognize that feature?"

"He was in attendance, too. We spoke of the saffron fields at the time. Lorenzo and I did love to exchange ideas."

They gazed at one another. "Then I must take this key and this dress and find that tower," Gabriela said.

"So it seems. At the base of that tower, you will find the chapel where the wedding I mentioned was performed. I will go with you. We will leave at daybreak."

"You are permitted into the world?"

The abbess turned toward the window. "Our order celebrates industry and must descend into the world to help the poor and to do our business dealings. Like everything our Medici patron did, the choice to send you to me has been well considered. Do you know the nature of what we seek?"

"Ancient books, manuscripts, codexes of some rarity, is my belief. Magnifico feared that all writing of a secular nature might be destroyed."

"And he was right to fear that."

"And you do not believe that pagan knowledge challenges Christianity?" Gabriela asked.

"I do not believe that our God is so easily threatened," came her reply. "Knowledge is not a threat as long as it remains in the hands of the good."

Brooke had a retort to that but Gabriela locked her down and sent her a furious thought: *I will acknowledge your presence when I have the opportunity, not now.*

It was only much later, after she had shared a meal in the refectory with the other sisters, that Gabriela shared with the abbess the existence of her inner voice.

"We all have an inner voice, Gabriela," Abbess Cosimato said as they walked together around the cloisters toward their cells. The evening air brushed across the herbs that grew in the gardens beyond and Gabriela deeply inhaled air scented with lavender and thyme. "Sometimes it is our angels providing us counsel and, for some, a much darker source."

"This is not the same kind of inner voice, Abbess. This one has a name, tells me of the future, and in truth, sounds far more human than divine. Her name is Brooke."

"Brooke?" The nun stopped and turned to face her. "Such a peculiar name."

"It is not of this world or of this century. Would you care to speak with her? She has been eager for conversation."

For a moment, Gabriela could see the thoughts flickering across the nun's face in the lamplight—concern, skepticism, perhaps fear, and finally curiosity followed by the abbess crossing herself. "By all means. Permit me to speak with this Brooke."

Thank you, Gabriela!

"I must warn you, Mother: my inner voice can be tiresome as well as strange in terms of diction."

And the voice of the future rose to Gabriela's lips with her usual audaciousness. "Never for a minute would I ever have thought that nuns were among our first feminists," Brooke began, "but now I see how you've carved a life of independence and creativity here in this sanctuary."

"Under the guidance of our Lord," the nun said, genuflecting and bowing before a cross on the wall and adding a Hail Mary for good measure. "And what pray tell is a feminist?"

"Someone who believes women have historically and politically been suppressed in the name of male authority, often using religion as the club with which to wield power. Look at how we've been subverted, relegated to servants to men in every possible way."

"Some would argue that that is due to Original Sin beginning with Eve and the Garden of Eden," Mother Superior posited.

"Original Sin? How can sin ever be original? That's another human construct, and why couldn't Adam be solely responsible for his own act? Eve offered him knowledge, something humanity craved. Oh, and why were the gospels of Mary Magdalene subverted by the male apostles in the first place?"

And on it went, both sides diving into a lively theological debate, though, admittedly, Brooke lacked the thorough knowledge of the scriptures that the abbess possessed. Still, before the evening was through and the body she shared with Gabriela demanded sleep, Brooke and Mother Cosimato realized that they stood firm on the same side, though the nun held tight to certain Biblical decrees upon which they agreed to disagree.

"You are exhausting," Gabriela remarked before she fell asleep in her cell that night, but regardless of her frustration with her alter ego, she nevertheless felt vibrantly alive in a way she had once feared would never return.

The morning dawned bright and clear when the small party of the Order of Saint Clare set off in a wagon for the countryside. Gabriela wore a habit as part of her disguise, and other than to imagine how she might embellish its dull expanse—a flight of tiny yellow birds along the hem, a mantle of glowing bronze velvet?—she was content enough. After all, at the end of this journey she would both end her quest, learn her father's fate, and possibly see her beloved Fili again.

The party of four nuns, the abbess, and Gabriela traveled in a large wagon drawn by two dray horses, the back filled with baskets of food, herbs, and bolts of cloth. The sisters took turns either walking or riding in the wagon, the abbess included. Wherever they went, they dispensed food and drink, made several stops in the small villages to tend the sick, and spent the first night as guests at another convent along the way. Once they paused at a church not only to pray but to deliver an altar cloth that had been created as a commission by their convent. The priest was so filled with joy at the sight of the gold embroidered cross on the field of green velvet that he fell to his knees to give thanks to God.

Along the way, the sisters chatted, laughed, pointed out this flower and that. Sister Ametto sketched wherever they went while Gabriela shared her ideas on design, color, and stitchery with Sister Nero. The camaraderie was addictive, like a warm cloak wrapped around the shoulders on a chill winter night. She had no idea how deeply she had missed the company of women.

Brooke remained deep within Gabriela, watching all with mounting anticipation but only commenting occasionally at something one of the sisters said.

The walled hamlet appeared on a hill late the second day, the crenellated tower that overlooked the land appearing just as Gabriela's sleeves had depicted: between an orchard and a field, both currently not in bloom. She sat in silence as the horses plodded up the track toward the community and said nothing when all the sisters climbed out to lighten the beasts' load.

Are you afraid of what you may find? Brooke asked.

I am but I am equally afraid of what I may not, Gabriela answered.

The tower bells rang out a welcome as they approached and the thick oaken gates were flung open for the villagers to dash down to greet them with much hand clasping and broad smiles. Such visitors were always welcome in these villages, sisters especially so as they brought news, medicines, and more.

Crossing himself while dipping a bow, one fellow stood out to introduce himself. "Welcome, sisters and holy abbess. We are most honored to have you as our guests at the Castello Garbino. My name is Signore Leo Travaldineri, the head man of the town, but I regret to say that Lord Corsi and his family have journeyed to Rome and are currently not home."

"No matter, Signore Travaldineri. Though we had hoped to see the lord, in truth we have come for quite another reason. We asked that you permit myself and another of our party to visit the tower."

"The tower?" The man's eyes widened in his round face sending his multiple chins spreading around his neck. "But of course, though I confess that there is nothing much of note there except the vista. I thought you had come to see the chapel."

"We will visit that, too, but also relish the view of God's good earth."

"Excellent!" Travaldineri clapped his hands together. "Meanwhile I will fetch the priest, who will be happy to know you have come. We are most proud of our chapel in these parts. I thought for certain that was the reason for your visit. One moment." He called to one of the boys encircling the group in eager watchfulness and sent him scurrying down the lane.

The abbess and Gabriela proceeded up the lane with Signore Travaldineri, a trail of children skipping eagerly behind calling out questions that either Gabriela or the abbess answered.

"Where do you live? Is it pretty?"

"We live many leagues away," the abbess said with a laugh, "and yes, it is very pretty."

"Arla, children, stop the chattering. Do not pester our esteemed guests," Signore Travaldineri chastised, but the abbess hastened to tell him that it was no bother at all and so the youngsters' questions continued right up the lane, past the little stone houses where women waved and smiled from their doorways, and up to the stoop of the tower.

Gabriela stared at the thick cedar hobnailed door, one hand grasping that of a little girl no older than six, the other gripping the key in her pocket. "It is locked?"

"Yes, yes," Signore Travaldineri assured her, "but only to keep the children out lest they climb up and hurt themselves."

He pulled a heavy iron key from his waist purse and Gabriela could see at a glance that hers was dwarfed by comparison. She kept it gripped in her fist.

Inside, the tower was much as she expected, a tall rectangle of stone with a dark narrow circular stairway climbing up and up. Travaldineri remained below citing breathing problems but sent his two guests up in the company of a youth named Rocco, the bell boy, who carried a lantern and said not a word unless spoken to.

After they had arrived at the topmost level and gazed out over the countryside, out of breath but no less exhilarated, the abbess sat on a stone bench leaving Gabriela to study the surrounding structure. Overhead hung three bronze bells, their ropes dangling down, and on all four sides square openings let in the air. A plain enough structure but one need not be a builder to note how the staircase seemed to hug the front of the tower leaving a considerable expanse of space at the rear.

You could easily tuck a hidden room in here and no one would give it a second thought, Brooke said.

My thinking, too, Gabriela thought back. "But where fits my key?" she said aloud.

"I wondered that," the abbess said. "Perhaps it is not to be found here. Let us descend now and view the chapel as the headman seems most proud of it. Rocco, lead the way, please."

Back at ground level, Signore Travaldineri awaited them eagerly. "Did you enjoy the vista?" he asked as he led them up the path.

"Indeed. It was lovely," the abbess told him, causing the man's smile to beam even brighter.

Before the door of the small chapel, they paused, and again Gabriela watched a key emerge that was also much larger and coarser than the one she had been given.

"Wait here one moment, please."

Puzzled, Gabriela and the abbess stood by while the headman entered, sending two older children ahead to light the candles. Once the church was illuminated, he called them in.

Gabriela stepped in and gasped. At first she focused on the small stained-glass rondel fixed above the nave, the only source of natural light, before taking in a simple stone chapel with its single nave and wooden trussed ceiling. But then the walls seemed to open up around her in a glowing world of color and pattern. Every inch of wall from either side of the door up to the altar had been covered in brilliant frescos. Angels and saints below, Mary and Jesus above, plus a gathering of richly robed citizens making a procession along the lower walls toward the front of the church.

Gabriela could not speak. It took a moment for the explosion of color and image surrounding her to settle into detail her eyes needed to explore. Then it was as if she gazed upon her own history, both in truth and that born of her imagination. Every one she knew and loved were there, gathered in finery of hers and her father's making, Florentine citizens, rich and poor. She recognized the ermine-lined robed man bearing a gift of a gilded box as Lorenzo de' Medici was attended by his wife, Lady Clarice, and his mother, Lady Lucrezia, but their neighbors at the Ognissanti, like the baker man Signore Ricardi and his wife, Anna, were there with others, too. Clients, friends, patrons—they were all in attendance moving forward with joyful expressions. To her right Sandro himself appeared to smile directly at her while holding her profile painting framed within his hands. She could see her mother standing in the crowd, too, her gaze washed with such loving pride and looking so real that Gabriela longed to run into her arms.

"It is a wedding," the abbess marveled. "Look to the altar, Gabriela."

There standing in profile beneath a canopy of painted angels stood a young woman in a shimmering velvet dress. Straight-backed, hands folded demurely over her waist, and wearing a magnificent gold-embossed giornea over a sleeveless gown of shimmering cream silk, the young woman did not suppress her blooming smile. One exquisite sleeve turned toward the viewer in an intricate play of triangular motifs embroidered and accented with pearls. Beside her stood a young man holding her hand wearing a rich blue velvet cioppa embossed at the neck and a red square hat on his head, his eyes luminous as he gazed upon his bride.

"It is my wedding!" Gabriela whispered, her feet moving as if by themselves toward the altar. The paint was so fresh it could not have been completed that long ago and obviously executed by a master painter who now stood with her at the altar. "Fili! Fili painted this, dear Fili. I recognize his style!"

She stopped short to gaze at the bridal pair, taking in every detail, overwhelmed with a burden of joy tangled with loss. How she wanted to reach out and touch the man's hand, feel his warmth, know he stood with her in the flesh instead of just his image. But this glorious wedding party was just a symbol, the whole procession of the living and the dead, a celebration of love and friendship that must exist in the realm of her dreams but never in the harsh light of the immediate moment.

But this commemorative is even more special, Brooke said. *Think of it as a memory because, once time passes, that's all we are left with, anyway. Here you are celebrated for your achievements, for all you are as a person, a woman, and as a designer, while everybody who loves or loved you gazes on. Your Filippino has given you the greatest gift ever.*

"Gabriela."

She turned to see the abbess standing behind her. "We will leave you to solitude for a time, surrounded by all your friends. Do not rush. We will be staying the night so take your time."

"Thank you." Gabriela turned back to her wedding painting, hearing the sound of footsteps followed by the door clicking shut behind her.

Now she gazed about at the landscape surrounding her wedding party, at the gnarled trees in this strange fantastical forest. Fili would hide a meaning here, envisioning the world as full of magic as she chose to see it, a world where goddesses roamed the world, flowers threaded through their tresses, petals strewn at their feet. And there, far away among the rolling hills, she could see stacks of books tucked away under rocks, branches growing out from the pages, like knowledge growing forth from the minds of men—everything vivid, alive, unconstrained. Her gifts, all of it.

"Oh, Fili," she whispered. "Thank you, and thank you for inviting—" she hesitated "—everybody." Because along with Jesus, Saint Francis of Assisi, the angel Gabriel, and assorted cherubs, he had added Zephyr and Flora to the guest list along with Venus running through a field of flowers with Mars swooping down from above as if late for an assignation. She stifled a laugh only for as long as she could hold it in before tears of joy mingled with tears of mirth and she collapsed in a pew laughing and crying both.

She was unsure of how long she remained that way but her hitched sobs shielded the sound of the door opening and the footsteps that followed.

"Gabriela?"

Swinging around, she stared into aisle behind her. The shape of a priest in a long black robe stood in the candlelight. "Father?"

16

*N*ot just a father but *her* father.

The sight of him was almost too much. He moved to sit beside her, shooing her inches across the oaken seat to make room for him. Taking her hand in his, he squeezed her fingers. "Dear Gabriela, I have waited so long for this moment."

"You are a priest when I thought you were dead? You could have…sent word." In truth she was so overjoyed to see him that none of that mattered.

"I could not," he assured her. "I came here in secret at Medici's request, delivering his treasure to safety as was the plan. Had I sent word, the message could have been traced or intercepted, the messengers tortured or worse, so I was to wait until you followed the clues to join me. Filippino remained here for at least part of that time, coming by in intervals to prepare the chapel for your wedding."

"Such a wedding." Gabriela gazed again at her procession.

"When we heard word from Lord Corsi that the Medici prodigy, Gabriela, had married her father's apprentice and that Jacopo Sistine had proclaimed himself head of the House of Domenico, I knew it was too late to return, that it must be up to you to stage an escape."

"He forced me to marry him," she said between hitching breaths, "kept me locked inside like some beast of burden, forbid me to design or sew or do anything of worth while he attempted to put me with child. I broke free only when Savonarola burned beauty in the streets and my supposed husband participated in the travesty. I saw him in the piazza that night, his arms full of my dresses gripping Mama's necklace—all which he considered his to do with as he pleased. I can never return, Father."

"Of course not. How did you escape?"

"The house finally emptied of my guards and I broke free that night. Sandro helped me escape Florence."

"God bless him," her father said with vehemence. "I would curse Jacopo had I the will. The man I had been would have stormed back to Florence to oust the upstart from my house and kick him into the street for treating you so but, in truth, you became his on the day you were wed. Nothing I could do would change a thing except to cause you more misery since his suffering would become yours. Instead, when I heard the news, I remained here, took my vows so I could tend to the needs of this parish, and make amends for my ways."

"Make amends for what?" she asked, turning to him. "You did what you thought best for your daughter and the will of your patron. Your apprentice upon whom you laid so much faith was the feckless one, not you, Father."

"I still abandoned you, though Magnifico promised to protect you should you choose to leave and I believe he did all within his power. But my pain goes back even further, back to the death of your mother. Ours was a love match, and when she died, a little bit of me went with her. I lost a taste for design, fashioning fine clothes for the wealthy turned me sour. When I arrived here and glimpsed another way of life—simpler, more true—I decided never to return to Florence. Forgive me."

"Of course I forgive you, Father, but what of the Magnifico's treasure?"

"Now locked away in a secret place until once again it is safe to unleash the knowledge it contains."

"The tower?"

He turned. "How did you know?"

Gabriela smiled. "I hold the clues in my sleeve, remember? I have brought the dress but now do not know what will become of it since my wedding is...over."

"Sell it to Lady Corsi."

Gabriela shook her head. "No. I will take it with me wherever I go and think how to refashion it as time goes on. But what of the key?" She pulled it from her pocket. "What of this?" She held the filigreed object up to the candle-light, turning it in her fingers this way and that. "I thought that it must open the secret cache of Medici treasure or release the final clue but now I think not."

"No, I think not." Her father took the key and continued holding it aloft. "To Lorenzo de' Medici, the key represented knowledge to which he opened to you through his tutor and the use of his library. He confessed to me once that you were a more able student than any of his own children and he thought of you as a daughter. I was foolish and annoyed by this as I wanted you at home and thought of you as solely my own but I was wrong to think so. In the end, we worked out an agreement. His wish was to gift you a grand wedding to the man you loved but even the great Magnifico could not control fate."

"No, he could not and yet in a way he has succeeded." She smiled around at her wedding guests. "He has given me a great gift in learning and my Fili gave me quite another."

After Gabriela pocketed the key, her father took both his hands in hers and held them tight. "You could stay with me, dearest, be my housekeeper, if you will. My cottage is simple but comfortable and I believe you would find peace here. I have a letter for you from Filippino, which may further your decision." He reached into his cassock and removed a piece of folded parchment sealed with the wax image of an open book. "I know some of the contents but not all. The man is private in many ways."

Gabriela stared down at the envelope, savoring the moment before breaking the seal and committing the contents to her heart. Taking the letter in hand, she left her father's side to stand before her heart's intended, whose likeness he had painted with his usual perfection.

DEAREST GABRIELA,

IF THE MOMENT of your reading this you are standing in the chapel surrounded by our beloved guests at the wedding of our true hearts, then I hope it is because you have escaped Jacopo at last. If this be true, know that the choice for your future is yours alone. I give you my heart. We have wed here in this chapel, our souls joined before God with this fresco as our testament. Know that I will never wed another. If you choose to join me, I will come to you here in this village and we will be together in the flesh. If you choose another path, I will understand.

You will have my heart always,
Your beloved Filippino Lippi

. . .

GABRIELA'S FATHER stepped up behind her, placing a hand on her shoulder. "My child, Filippino knows better than most how the life of an artist's wife is punishing. Having been born the son of Fra Filippo Lippi and the fallen nun, he watched his mother suffer—often left alone while his artist father traveled to commissions leaving his wife behind as a victim of jests and cruel remarks. As you are already wed to another, he fears that it could be likewise for you, unbearable even if you were to hide, which you certainly must. It is not a fate he wishes for you. Still, I agreed to have you stay with me until he arrives and however long thereafter. Whatever you decide, I will support. Stay with me forever or go with him. Either way, it is not me but God who will judge you."

Her eyes met his.

God doesn't judge you, people do, Brooke told her.

"We judge ourselves first," Gabriela said aloud, "whether it is God within us that decides, I do not know."

"Gabriela, what are you saying?" her father asked.

"That I have made my decision. Filippino and I often spoke of our joy in making art, how creation brings us that much closer to God. Once all the seconds are removed from the days and time stands still, that is when God touches us most deeply. I must find my own way."

"I do not understand, my dear."

"Every person must find their own path. They will not be the same. My time to be a wife has passed and I have no will to follow another." She spread her hands. "Filippino has given me the wedding of my dreams, which I will hold in my heart forever. Magnifico and you, dear father, have given me knowledge and so much more. I will hold you all in my heart as I take another path."

"What is it you are saying, Gabriela?" her father asked again.

"I will return with the sisters of the Order of Saint Clare where I will apply the gifts I have been given in the company of my sisters. I will be content, perhaps even joyful. In my heart, I know I have loved and wed but now I must move on."

And so must I, Brooke said.

I know it, came Gabriela's reply. *But we will be together always.*

Brooke made to send another thought but already the brilliant frescos had begun to slip away, replaced by gray interspersed with cubes of color, leaving her standing with her hands clasped in Enrico's, her eyes filled with tears.

For a moment the world was still, Enrico's eyes fixed on hers as if struggling to grapple with the abrupt shift. "She released you?" he asked at last.

"We released each other," Brooke told him, dropping her hands so she could wipe her eyes. "We both knew that it was time. We're free now and yet I believe our two souls are fused forever, maybe even healed somehow."

"She became a nun, seriously?" Felix said behind her.

"She became an *artist*," Brooke countered, turning. "She found the one place in her world that allowed a woman freedom to create while offering her companionship and a life free from servitude. Maybe not all orders were like this and I'm sure many were like prisons of another sort but she didn't see serving God as servitude, anyway. She came from a world that called on all citizens to pray, so she was more than prepared for that than perhaps we would be today. In the end, all I could feel in her heart was gratitude...and love, even excitement. Her fingers itched to pick up the needle, to draw thread again."

"I thought for certain that she would die, meet a horrible end, and then you would endure her pain in her final hours, dear Brooke," Stephani said on her other side, her grin wide with relief. "And yet here you are, returned to us whole at last."

Brooke smiled across at her. "That was my fear, too, but in the end she found the peace she needed and the opportunity to create what she craved. Though we were so different in so many ways, in that we were one. Now I feel as though the world has opened up for me to pursue my creativity to the fullest extent and finally live my own life, too."

"How marvelous to hear. Now, let me show you something. I have been engaged in research while your journey has been unfolding," Stephani said. "It began when I remembered a piece I read not long ago about the Uffizi's recent acquisition of a newly discovered Botticelli portrait. Look what I discovered." She held up her tablet to the profile of a young woman wearing extraordinary sleeves. "I recognized her at once."

"That's her," Brooke cried, "That's Gabriela's portrait, Botticelli's wedding gift to her and Filippino! But where was it found?"

"Ah." Stephani nodded. "There is quite a story there, as it happens. Have you heard of a Phoebe McCabe and the Agency of the Ancient Lost and Found?"

Brooke's blank look said it all.

"No matter, but let me just say that this is not the only discovery made by the group. The portrait led to a Tuscan winery where a tower library has remained in the care of the Corsi family for centuries and look what they found in the chapel." Swiping the tablet to the right, she brought up the photo of a stunning, though badly damaged, fresco.

"Oh, my God, look at that!" Enrico exclaimed. "That is it! Gabriela's wedding picture has been found!"

Brooke's legs gave out. Felix helped her to the nearest chair. "I can't believe it," she whispered, "to see it so faded and damaged after just witnessing the work in all its splendor."

"It was only five centuries ago, after all," Enrico whispered, equally overcome.

"We must go," Brooke said.

"Of course we must," Stephani agreed.

"In the meantime, what about the dress?" Felix asked, holding up the glowing golden fabric caught in a sunbeam pouring down from one of the upper windows.

Brooke gazed at the loveliness of silk and velvet catching the deeper tones in the creases as it flowed to the floor. "That's where Gabriela and I will always meet, the two of us caught like...a spirit in the fold."

The End

AFTERWORD

Renaissance Florence was not a good time to be a woman. Historically, one can easily argue that there are few good times to be a woman, but why even then, in this city of light and learning, when the Renaissance was witnessing such a great explosion of art and literature, were half of the population still cloistered? The short answer is religion, specifically the male dictates of the Catholic church.

When I started on Gabriela's journey, my research led me to surprising places. Not being Catholic, I had much to learn, and trying to place myself in the mind of one who grew up believing absolutely in the literal interpretation of the Bible was a revelation. And yet many thinkers of the time were questioning the dogma, some among the faithful themselves.

That Gabriela eventually finds her freedom in the church was a total revelation. I had no idea that certain convents were the feminist powerhouses of the Renaissance while still adhering to the dictates of the Roman Catholic church. In the end, it's all a matter of perspective, faith, and belief, and how each of us find our way to the light, by whatever name we choose. By the end of my research on Renaissance womanhood, let me just say that going to a convent did not seem like such a dire fate.

Printed in Great Britain
by Amazon

77869739R00088